Ring o' Roses

After a year spent in Canada, Cathy Maitland returns to England to be bridesmaid at the wedding of her old school friend, Ruth. The best man having slipped a disc, Ruth's elder brother, Joss, is persuaded to take his place and that evening, when Cathy and Joss meet after the reception, they find that their feelings for each other have changed completely. Instead of their former indifference, each experiences a new and overwhelming attraction to the other.

On her return to St Martha's Hospital the following Monday Cathy finds that because of a 'flu epidemic she has been transferred to the Accident Unit, where Joss is already working as acting S.A.O. But, although this seems a happy coincidence, things just don't work out as expected, and against a background of crisis and emergency a dedicated team have to cope not only with human tragedy and suffering, but with the problems of their own tangled relationships. Finally, though, a passionate quarrel forces Cathy and Joss to express their true feelings and, by putting right their misunderstandings, both are able to find the happiness for which they are looking.

In Ring o' Roses *Lucilla Andrews has created yet another masterly hospital story, full of the emotion, wit and excitement that have become her trademark and earned for her such a high reputation among successful novelists.*

Further Titles by Lucilla Andrews from Severn House

ENDEL HOUSE
THE FIRST YEAR
MARSH BLOOD

RING O'ROSES

Lucilla Andrews

This edition published in Great Britain 1994 by
SEVERN HOUSE PUBLISHERS LTD of
9–15 High Street, Sutton, Surrey SM1 1DF.
First published in Great Britain 1972 by George G Harrap & Co. Ltd.

British Library Cataloguing in Publication Data
Andrews, Lucilla
  Ring O'Roses. – New ed
  I. Title
  823.914 [F]

  ISBN 0-7278-4631-0

For Alison and Hector

Typeset by Hewer Text Composition Services, Edinburgh.
Printed and bound in Great Britain by
Redwood Books, Trowbridge, Wiltshire.

Chapter One

The Cross of St George was flying from the square tower of the old grey church that afternoon. The lilac bushes by the church were purple, white and blue-mauve; and in the banks of the lane running up from the village, there were bluebells, buttercups and early cow parsley. I had remembered the wild flowers, but forgotten the grass was so green.

'Young Ruth can't grumble for her wedding.' Bert Mercer pushed up the peak of the tweed cap he had worn during the seven years Ruth and I travelled in his school taxi. 'Bridesmaid, aren't you? You'll be on time. The ringers are still down the Lamb.' He turned into the vicarage drive. 'Been on your holidays, have you?'

'I'm just finishing one. Back to work on Monday.'

His blue eyes considered me calmly as he braked. 'London?' I nodded. 'Didn't fancy Canada same as your mum and brother, then?'

I avoided looking at the house next door. The two houses stood alone on the hilltop and opposite the church. 'I enjoyed working there this last year. A beautiful country.'

'That's nice.' He glanced at that other house. 'Could've done with your dad last winter. Me chest was playing up again. This new young chap gives me these tablets and says to stay off the spirits. Won't mix, he says. Tablets!' He snorted. 'That's all these young doctors know, seemly. Your dad wouldn't have given me no tablets. He'd have fetched me down a bottle of his linctus, told the wife to tuck me off with a hot toddy, I'd have sweated it out and been back on the school run in the week! Three weeks I had on the club with them tablets! How was I to know as he meant to stay off the beer? Didn't say, did he? Missed your dad, I can tell you! You didn't catch him telling a working man to stay off his beer.' He heaved himself out and lunged into the back for my bags. 'When did you get back from Canada, then?'

I smiled. 'Just over two hours ago. I was due yesterday but our flight was delayed by a snowstorm in Montreal.'

Bert Mercer and his ancestors came from the village at the foot of that hill. The village had seen the Romans arrive and leave; the Jutes burn it down; the Normans take it over; the Battle of Britain overhead and a fair selection of World War II bombs fall on and around it. The village could show emotion, when very drunk. 'Snow, eh?' Bert shoved up his cap another inch. 'Wouldn't fancy it this time of the year meself, neither.'

'Cathy, dear! Welcome back!' Mrs Desmond exploded through her front door, kissed me warmly and re-skewered her hat. 'Bert, will you kindly leave those bags just inside the door and go back to the next train—splendid!' She ushered me into the transformed vicarage hall, round caterers and trestle tables, to the foot of the main stairs. 'You'll find everything waiting in the guest-room—next to the guest-room—next to the old school-room—remember? You won't mind if I leave you, dear? Ruth's having a little trouble with her veil—she's a bit edgy—bride's prerogative, as I've told her! But she was quite relieved when you rang from the airport as she did find yesterday a little trying. Of course, the best man's slipping a disc was rather unfortunate—'

6

'Nigel Jarvis?' I exclaimed. 'Ruth didn't tell me on the—'

'As I've said, dear—we are a bit edgy! The poor boy came off his tractor, but as he's not badly hurt and the tractor skidded on alone into a half-empty dyke and was quite undamaged, really we can only be thankful. Tractors are so precious at this season! Not too travel-worn? Good! Off you go! The Vicar and Danny have already gone across to the church and we mustn't be too long.' She waved me up the stairs as if it were five minutes, not over three years, since I had last been in her house. Nor, despite a new cream straw sombrero and navy silk outfit, did she look in any way altered. She had always been a large handsome woman with a weakness for huge hats and the engrained air of being about to declare the bazaar open.

I was very fond of Mrs Desmond. She was so genuinely kind and had a lack of imagination I had found restful as a child. Being incapable of visualizing the worst, Mrs Desmond had waited until one fell out of a tree before putting it out of bounds. My mother had only to see a child glance at a tree to see a broken back. In Mrs Desmond's place now, my mother would be convinced the dress made to measurements exchanged across the Atlantic would never fit me; she would take the best man's accident as a bad omen that must inevitably herald the bridegroom's breaking his neck before he reached the church, or the Vicar's suffering a stroke from the emotional strain of marrying his favourite child to a man taking her to Australia for two years directly after the honeymoon.

My brother had mother's temperament. 'How can you stand going back? It'll be agony!' both had assured me constantly for the last month. Being even less sure now than then that I could stand it, once the anaesthetizing effect of my post-flying hangover wore off, I was very grateful to have been sent up to get changed alone before

7

even seeing Ruth. The mental breathing space was such perfect therapy that for the first time in my life I wondered if Mrs Desmond was as unimaginative as we had all assumed, or if thirty years of marriage to a theological scholar with a dry sense of humour and very High Church leanings in a country living where, irrespective of social backgrounds, all three qualities were regarded with deep suspicion, was responsible for her reputation for seeing only the silver linings. She was a very popular as well as very good Vicar's wife.

The long powder-blue velvet dress, matching shoes and gloves fitted exactly. The hair ribbon was the right length. I studied the result in the long mirror and tried unsuccessfully to accept the pallid blonde zombie staring back as myself. Her ability to stand still was no help as I was now back to feeling the sway of the 'plane. It was like being suspended on the end of a piece of string held by eternity with a childish streak. Just as one grew accustomed to the sway, eternity twitched it up or dropped it down.

A knock on the door startled me disproportionally. I opened it carefully as a drunk and blinked at the man in a morning suit holding a posy of cornflowers and pink roses. 'You look different, Joss,' I said.

He was Ruth's elder brother and was smiling rather nicely. 'So do you, Cathy. Very charming but not yet with us. Why don't you sit down?'

I backed and sat on the bed. 'It isn't lack of food. They fed us all night.'

'Just time-lag.' He gave me the posy, explained he had taken over as best man and driven up with it as it had been accidentally delivered to the bridegroom's home. 'The ringers were staggering out of the Lamb as I came by. I must get back before they start or poor Tom'll blow another gasket.'

'Poor Tom. Poor Nigel. Your mother says he's not too bad.'

8

'Just cursing his guts out at doing this at this time of year.' He asked after my mother, brother and sister-in-law but tactfully omitted my step-father.

I said, 'He's a very nice man, Joss. I didn't expect to like him, but I do, very much.'

'I'm glad on all counts,' he said, as if he meant it.

Ruth and I were the same age, twenty-four. Joss was five years older, Danny a year younger. As kids the five-year gap had been enough to cause Ruth and me irritation, without being sufficient to make us respect his being able to tie his own shoelaces, or buy himself a beer at the Lamb while we had to sit outside eating crisps and ducking behind parked cars when any member of the P.C.C. or Mothers' Union went by. All our childhood, Joss and I had accepted each other partly as we had no alternative and partly as we had managed to achieve a kind of undemanding but solid understanding that was firmly based on shared roots and mutual indifference.

The young Desmonds all had their father's dark hair and eyes, but only Joss their mother's heavier features and build. As a boy he had been all jaw, nose and triangular eyebrows, with bones that looked too big for him. We had last met at my father's funeral, but I could not now remember what he had then looked like. I had a dim recollection of his saying that if I ever wanted to look round another hospital, to give him a ring, he would show me round Benedict's and buy me a meal. I had not taken that up and nor had he done more about it. During the remaining years of my general training in St Martha's, London, I had seen Ruth regularly but neither of her brothers. I noticed absently Joss's bones no longer seemed too big and that my face seemed to be puzzling him. I asked what was wrong with it. 'Do I need more lipstick? Or have I forgotten to make up both eyes?'

'Turn to the light.' He came nearer, and being considerably taller than myself and standing, bent for a closer look. 'You'll do, as you are.' He stepped back rather quickly. 'See you.' He went out and closed the door. I got up quickly and looked at myself in the mirror. I was still wondering if I had imagined the expression I had seen flickering through Joss's eyes just now, when I chanced to look out of the window and forgot everything else. The window overlooked the back garden next door. The new owners had replaced my father's cherished rose beds with turf. I had just enough time to re-do my eyes before the bells started and Mrs Desmond called me to Ruth's room.

Ruth's Victorian-styled dress was of broderie anglaise and her long dark hair was piled up under a short lace veil. She was a very pretty, slim girl and she looked dreamy. We walked round each other in silence then began to laugh, wildly. Mrs Desmond beamed on us. 'There's nothing like a good laugh to settle the nerves,' she said.

Tom Everett, Ruth's bridegroom, had been in the fifth at our co-ed grammar when Ruth and I were first-formers. His father was owner-editor of the local paper and around that time had bought a house in the village. As Tom had fed us with some of the pastry from the meat pies he bought to eat on the journey home, with unusual charity we had named him Acne-Chops. One morning in his 'A' Level year he had appeared in Bert's taxi with a pipe. After we told him we thought a pipe did something for an older man, he had sucked it constantly in the taxi until he left school. He never lit it.

Ruth spluttered, 'He still doesn't smoke.'

'So wise,' said Mrs Desmond. 'I wish Danny would give it up.'

The pealing bells cascaded over the hill, the village below and the flat green farmland beyond when Mrs Desmond and I crossed the lane a few minutes later. The little group of women waiting by the lych-gate stepped aside. 'It's the old Doctor's girl! You remember poor Dr

Maitland—took bad just after evening surgery—gone he was, gone—before his poor wife could get a hand to the 'phone for the ambulance—cruel shock—and how are you then, dear? And your mum? So young Paul's got his-self a wife, eh? There! Your turn next, dear! Lovely day you got for your Ruth, eh, Mrs Desmond?'

The bells faded away but the birds went on singing. The sunshine filtering through the stained-glass windows sent shafts of red, blue and yellow onto white-washed walls that had been five hundred years old when Tudor England was middle-aged. Suddenly the faces swung round, some familiar, some strange, some appraising, some envying, some smiling. I only properly noticed Tom Everett's face. He looked quite incredibly happy.

This time: 'Dearly beloved we are gathered together . . .'

Last time: 'Man that is born of woman . . .' Was that the last time? Hadn't I been here in the months before our house sold? If I had, I couldn't remember. I couldn't even remember the two family weddings I had attended in this last year.

'We're on the move, Cathy,' murmured Joss.

In the vestry he drew my hand through his arm as we formed up behind the parents and asked very quietly if I thought the final hymn had been a strictly tactful choice.

'What was it?'

'Now thank we all our God.' His eyes smiled into mine. 'Take it easy. You sang the official version, not the bawdy variation you wrote after 'O' Levels.'

'I'd forgotten that.' I smiled back as we followed the little procession down the aisle.

A battery of professional and amateur photographers was waiting outside the church. We were grouped and regrouped. 'Bride and her mother alone, please . . . bride and bridesmaid . . . cheese, ladies, cheese, please . . . bride and groom again. . . .'

The front gate of our old house looked naked without the brass plate. The flowering current bushes in the front garden had been replaced by ailing rhododendrons. They wouldn't do well in that soil. Too much lime. 'Nothing'll do well in the wrong soil,' my father said.

Canada had been wrong for me. I had not been able to say that to my family as it would have hurt them too much. With the enthusiasm of converts and the self-exiled's need for justification, they saw in black and white. Canada was their Promised Land, England all strikes, scruffy students, drugs. 'Why go back?'

Simply, I had missed England. When my training ended, I had taken a year's job in a Canadian hospital to see if my mother was as content as she seemed from her letters. She was more than that, she was happy. After her re-marriage three months ago I wrote to the Chief Nursing Officer at Martha's. She had answered by return, offering me the job of Senior Staff Nurse in Luke Ward. 'After so much departmental surgery,' she wrote, 'I think you will enjoy a return to medical nursing.'

Tomorrow I was due back at my old digs in London. Yesterday I had been sorry my weekend with the Desmonds would be cut short. I liked them all, but I wasn't sorry now my flying hangover was wearing much thinner. It was too early yet to tell whether or not coming back was a mistake, but not that parts of it hurt like hell.

Particularly the reception. At first.

'Cathy, I want all your news! My dear, it seems so strange not having the Maitlands on this hill. I expect you're quite sad to see the old house again?'

'Drink up, girl,' said Joss. 'I'm tired of toting this full bottle.'

'So your dear mother has re-married, Cathy? I always thought she was so devoted—but they say he's a wealthy man? Not that he can take your father's place in your heart—I know just how you feel, dear—'

12

'Cathy, you can't imagine how we miss your father! He was such a good doctor—he'd come out in any weather at any hour—I expect you miss him still?'

'Let's have your glass, Cathy,' said Joss.

'Cathy, I can't wait to hear all your news! But, darling —have you heard about our railway? They're trying to take it away, so we've formed an Action Group. . . .'

Suddenly, it was over. Slowly, the cars disgorged from the Glebe Field; the caterers began stacking glasses, folding cloths; the parents and elder relatives retreated to the Vicar's study before their dinner with the Everett seniors; Danny started organizing our party. Danny was now taller and thinner than Joss, with his better-looking face hidden by a thick black beard.

I had to have quiet. I drifted out to the vegetable garden and sat on the bench against a wall. It was too far from the house for the voices on the front lawn to be more than a distant babble weaving into the background hum of tractors. On any fine Saturday at this time of the year, that hum lasted as long as the light. The air smelt as it always had; of new-cut grass, new-turned earth, diesel, lilac, and faintly of salt from the sea eleven miles away. My travel fatigue had gone, but thanks to the champagne I looked at our old house with nothing more than an affectionate incredulity that it should still be there, without us.

Joss joined me so silently that I was unaware of the fact until he sat down. We exchanged smiles in a silence that picked up old threads far more tangibly than words. It had the unstrained quality only possible between old friends on the same wavelength and was as soothing as my former solitude. But watching him staring at nothing, I was amused to find myself thinking that had we only met today, this particular silence would have been the last thing I would have expected, or maybe even wanted from him. For the first time I understood why my local

13

girl-friends used to envy my treating the vicarage as a second home and grumble at the waste of the best bit of local talent, when Joss brought home his dates from Cambridge, and later as a medic. student from Benedict's. The stream stopped once he was a houseman as then he seldom got home and when he did, he slept. When our house was sold he had been a junior surgical registrar at Benedict's, with even less free time. Occasionally, in London, Ruth had mentioned him in connection with some girl, but in her letters this last year, only under the general 'the family are all flourishing'. I wondered vaguely about his present sex life, and then with more interest why every old friend over thirty-five this afternoon had asked when I was going to find myself a husband and been so annoyed by my truthful reply that I was in no hurry to marry.

'So many of you girls say that these days! You know your trouble? Too much freedom, too much money, and you mustn't mind my adding, too irresponsible!'

I had let that go with a weak smile since none of the speakers had worked in a hospital and someone, generally Joss, kept refilling my glass.

He roused himself to ask how I felt about Danny's rave. 'Too tired to face it?'

'No, but when I helped Ruth into her going-away gear she told me you only got down this morning. On call last night?' He nodded, watching me thoughtfully. 'Are you?'

'Not too tired, but too old. I'd much prefer us to opt out for a civilized meal somewhere on our own. How about it?'

I hesitated, though I was in no mood for another party. 'Joss, I know you're officially lumbered with me—'

'And you with me, darling. If you can stand the strain a bit longer, I'll continue to enjoy it.' His expression was surprisingly kind. 'Been very hellish?'

I shook my head. 'Mainly thanks to all the champagne

14

you've been pouring into me. Anyway, I realized people meant to be kind—'

'Dear old chums.' He grimaced. 'Theirs is "the loving kindness that is pity's kin—and is most pitiless." What's the verdict?'

'I'd much rather dine with you. Thanks for the invitation and kind thought.'

He stood up and held out a hand. 'Darling, you've been living too long amongst the primitive colonials if you can now kid yourself any Englishman is ever prompted by kindness when he puts this proposition to a very pretty little dolly.'

I laughed and stood up. 'And will there be etchings on your lugger?'

'On home territory? Only a chastely framed copy of the Vicar's eldest lad's Union Rules. Hence all afternoon, one miserable glass of champagne.'

'Joshua! Such nobility!'

'Such craftiness! I hoped I'd be driving the lugger.'

We drove miles across the marsh to a newish road-house he said was good value. When the sun went down, the wide, empty sky was scarlet and gold; the wild roses in the low hedges were pale, ghostly; the cow parsley edged the flat green fields with white lace; and the dykes pointed long topaz fingers, seawards. The fat, omnipresent lambs were old enough to risk drowning as they slithered up and down the dyke banks, and everywhere the curlew rose in flapping black and white clouds.

I thought aloud. 'This was the kind of English evening that had the brain-drainers over the other side weeping into their Scotch or Bourbon.'

'I'd miss it.'

'I did.'

He slowed, then glanced at me. 'Would've had me back too. Many want to return?'

'Around sixty per cent of those I met would be back tomorrow if they weren't hooked on the lolly.'

'Understandable.' He drove on in silence for a little while. 'What was working and living over there really like, Cathy?'

We had finished dinner before I finished telling him and asked his news. 'The last I heard, you'd both parts of Fellowship and were running Benedict's Accident Unit. I remember, as that was when I went to ours. Still there?'

'No.' The way he was watching me through his thick dark lashes struck a forgotten chord. Half-closing his eyes when shy or nervous had been one of his mannerisms as a boy. 'I've crossed the river.'

'To Martha's'? I smiled widely. 'How? When? Why?'

'I answered an advert for Hoadley East's senior registrar. Six months ago. I wanted to work with him.'

'Joss, I'm impressed! You must be very good!' That was true. Sir Hoadley East was our senior consultant orthopaedic surgeon. Martha's Establishment was notoriously addicted to appointing Martha's men to Martha's jobs, no matter how well advertised. Any outsider who beat the system had to be demonstrably better than Martha's best. 'Congratulations,' I added.

'Thanks.' He pushed back his chair as the record player switched from ten-year-old pop to a Glenn Miller album. 'Come and dance to this soothing syrup before the good impression wears off—or are your feet killing you?'

I stood up. 'My feet are fine, thanks.'

'Good.' He held out his arms. 'We'll do a nice decorous turn around the floor.'

A few minutes later, he asked, 'When did we last dance together?'

I had to think. 'Before—before you went to Cambridge. You wanted to practise in the schoolroom. Didn't work out. You said I was too short for you.'

He brushed his chin over the top of my head. 'Not now. You've grown.'

I looked up. 'Not since I was thirteen, but you have.'

He smiled. 'A very young and foolish lad. I like your

16

scent. Handsome present from a well-heeled brain-drainer?'

'From my step-father.'

His hold tightened slightly. 'Very generous of you to wear it, Cathy.'

'I felt I should. He's being so good to Mum—and he insisted on paying my fare home. He's generous, plus.'

'Sounds a good chap.' He was briefly silent. 'Meet many Canadian good chaps?'

'Quite a few.'

'Husky, well-scrubbed, manly characters?'

'To a man.'

'Yet you came back?' He held me a little off to look at my face. 'Does this mean you prefer decadent Englishmen?'

I opened my eyes wide. 'I have this weakness for crumbling civilization.'

He drew me closer and rested his face on my hair. 'Rule Britannia.'

We danced in silence and extraordinarily well together until the record ended. ' "Come Dancing" ,' said Joss, 'must see us.' He breathed as if he had been running and we went back to our table without touching each other again, and tried to pretend that the dance had altered nothing. But the new tension between us was tangible as the dinner-table. As always when that happens, we were having two simultaneous conversations. Neither of us paid much attention to the one we put into words. Our silences grew more frequent and were as strained as that earlier one had been easy, for much the same basic reason.

The vicarage lights were on when we drove round to the garage behind the vegetable garden. Being so far from the house, once the garage light was off, momentarily the country darkness blinded my now unaccustomed eyes. A few hours back I would have grabbed for Joss. I grabbed for the garage door.

'Want a hand, Cathy?' He could have been a polite stranger, only had this been our first date a stranger would not now have had to ask that.

'Thanks.' I felt his hand reaching for mine, but very slowly. 'And for a splendid dinner, Joss.'

'Thank you. Can we *rep. mist.* some time? I'd like that very much.'

'I would, too.'

'Good.' He kissed my hand. 'How's the champagne?'

'Wedding or dinner?'

'Both.'

'Nicely assimilated by all that good food and coffee. How's yours?'

'Did you lace mine with vodka?'

'No.'

'Must be this moonlight,' he said and lightly kissed my lips.

I looked at the dark moonless sky as somewhere an owl hooted. 'How many times did you get called up last night?'

'I dunno.' His arms were round me and he began kissing me properly. 'Serendipity,' he murmured, 'that's the word I want.'

I was having even more difficulty in touching down than after the flight. 'For what?'

'The faculty of making happy and unexpected discoveries by accident. Cathy, this is bloody absurd—'

'Crazy. We should go in.'

'We should, but that's not what I meant.' His deep voice was unsteady. 'You've hit me so hard I can't think straight. All I can think is that I—hell—I think I bloody love you. Mind?'

I hadn't any breath for speech. I shook my head. He did not say anything or move for about two minutes. Then he said conversationally, 'You're right. Time to go in.'

The Vicar came out of the kitchen with a glass of milk

18

on a tray as we went in by the back door. 'Ah, there you are! Pleasant evening? Good, good. Your mother's rather tired so I'm just taking this up—oh yes, Joss—your hospital rang about an hour ago. Your Senior Surgical Officer asked if you would be good enough to ring him directly you got home. I hope this doesn't mean you'll have to leave us prematurely? I'll just take this up and be with you both, shortly.'

Joss and I had exchanged similar glances. After the Vicar vanished up the back stairs, I asked, 'This your free weekend?' He nodded dreamily. 'He can't want you to drive back tonight?'

'Your hospital, darling. Like to bet?'

I looked at the time. It was a quarter to one on Sunday morning and fifty miles from London. 'No.'

Joss raised both arms from his sides then let them fall in a gesture that was both triumphant and defeated. 'If it's not union rules, it's suffering humanity. Come and comfort me whilst I find out what's bugging Michael Roth, but I warn you—don't offer me an apple or a flagon as I don't fancy either!'

I took his offered hand. 'I won't.'

He rang from the Vicar's study. He had to drive back that night, as a man called Stan Lawson had a temperature of one hundred and three.

Chapter Two

Stan Lawson was Senior Accident Officer in our newish Accident Unit. In Martha's the job had the same status as the deputy Senior Surgical Officer, and was a yearly appointment open only to Fellows of the Royal College of Surgeons with at least six months full-time accident experience. It appealed only to a minority of individualists, owing to the irregular and generally very long hours, the necessity for making and acting on their own immediate decisions, and the professional vulnerability consequent on constant contact with a litigious general public.

Stan Lawson had been Junior Accident Officer when I worked in our A.U. up to leaving for Canada. When we said goodbye, he told me he intended applying for the job when the then S.A.O.'s contract ended. 'I'm thirty and I've been someone's stooge long enough. I want the buck.'

I wished him luck and said I hoped he would not collect the ulcers that seemed to go with that buck. He'd shrugged. 'There's no interesting job without massive problems, but at least, in the A.U., we're spared the super bloody problem bugging most of the human race—why am I in this business? Here we're in business to save healthy lives. I think that'll keep me off the tranquillizers.'

It was his weekend on and he had worked all day

feeling terrible but was too busy to do anything about it. When he got back to his flat, his wife, a junior ward sister, had taken his temperature, then rung the S.S.O. The latter told Joss Stan was the sixteenth member of the staff to go down with the new 'flu virus since Joss left that morning. 'Yesterday—two. Today—this! The S.M.O.'s being revoltingly smug. For the last two or three weeks, every time he's heard of the odd case in London he's said once it got a hold it would rip round like bloody dynamite. This is the new bug that hit the States a few months ago and as none of us here have met it, my learned opposite number says it won't surprise him if even the immunized pick it up. When not slapping himself on the back tonight, he's forecasting closed wards before the month's out. Ghoulish bastards, physicians. I'm sorry to do this to you, but I can't get hold of George Charlesworth [the J.A.O.] as he's spending his weekend touring. In any event, he hasn't enough experience yet to take over for more than a day or so. Can you make it tonight to move in first thing tomorrow? Today was a bloody shambles. If this weather lasts, tomorrow'll be worse.'

Joss rang off and linked his hands behind my waist. 'You get this bug across the water?'

'Me and two-thirds of the hospital. If it's the same, it's dynamite all right. Makes one feel like death before, during, and after.'

'Bundle of sunshine, aren't you, darling?' He kissed my neck. 'Wonder how many people Stan Lawson's handed it on to today.'

'I was wondering that. The invasion's very short. Poor Stan. This'll worry him a lot.'

'Chum of yours?'

'Just to work with. He's sweet—so's his wife. She's three years senior to me.' I held his face away. 'You met her?'

'No. I'm the new boy, remember? I've met old Stan. Decent chap. So's George Charlesworth.'

21

I smiled. 'There you're one up on me. I know his name, but I don't think I've ever seen him.'

'Quiet little man with glasses. I've heard he doesn't know much but learns fast.' He frowned to himself. 'I've also heard one of the three Unit staff nurses is particularly good but can't remember which.'

'How come you're such a mine of information on the A.U.? And who's Sister there now? Know that too?'

He grinned. 'Yep. A girl called Naomi Butler. Benedict's girl. We worked together in our Unit.'

'A Benedict's—' I laughed with him at my reaction. 'Just fancy!'

'And knowing your own hospital, how do you think they'll fancy this Benedict's take-over?'

'Oh—maybe just a complaint to the Race Relations Board.'

His triangular eyebrows shot up. 'Only that? No tar and feathers?'

I stopped smiling. 'Joss, have you had much of that?'

'The occasional dirty crack's inevitable if one muscles in on any enclosed community.'

'Do you dirty crack back?'

He laughed quietly. 'I just wear my Benedict's tie.'

'My dear man! Why haven't you been lynched? Got a death wish?'

'Oh no, my love,' he said in a different voice, 'oh no. So don't look at me like that, Cathy, or I'll be in danger of losing my job tonight.'

I backed rather breathlessly. 'I'll make you some tea whilst you change.'

'Tea?' The Vicar had joined us. 'I must say I'd enjoy a cup myself. You'll find your way round, Cathy? Splendid!'

Joss followed me into the hall. 'Thank God,' he said piously, 'there'll always be an England—just as long as there's a tea-leaf left.'

After he had gone the Vicar and I finished the pot in the

22

kitchen. Mr Desmond looked round the huge Victorian room as if seeing it for the first time. He was a slight, neat man with fine-drawn very regular features and thick grey hair. He looked ten years older than he had in church that afternoon. My father had been his great friend. We had exchanged general family news, but neither of us had mentioned either my father or Ruth. Danny was still out and the big house was very quiet.

He took off his glasses to rub his tired eyes. 'Parenthood, Cathy, is a blessed but disorientating experience.' He sighed. 'For around twenty years the uproar created by one's children frequently causes one to fear for one's sanity and eardrums—and then the silence becomes even more disturbing. Come and see us whenever you can spare the time.'

'Vicar, I'd love to. Thank you.'

'That will give Margaret great pleasure. She is going to miss—our daughter. And if, when you visit us, you'll kindly turn that lamentable record-player in the schoolroom to full volume and cause Margaret to protest you're disturbing my sermon, you'll be doing more than one act of charity.' His dark eyes smiled like Joss's. 'The Lord has given to me greatly, but in His wisdom omitted a talent for sermon-writing. Disturbed concentration has long provided an equally cogent excuse for my unfortunate parishioners and my ego.'

It was the longest conversation we had ever had, possibly as Ruth had always been around formerly and she talked as much as her mother. I was too tired that night to work out whether her marriage, or absence, had been the catalyst with him, or even what had happened between Joss and myself. I was merely conscious of a new and wholly unexpected joy simmering inside me exactly like water coming to boil in a kettle. The sensation lasted all weekend. Before I left Mrs Desmond echoed her husband's invitation and said how delighted she was that

Joss and I were working in the same hospital. 'Naturally, I realize St Martha's is a big place and you may not see much of each other, but I expect you'll manage to keep in touch, won't you?'

'I think we will,' I said, feeling a hideous—and enchanted—fraud.

My landlady gave me a tremendous welcome and the inside story on the new ground-floor lodgers. 'God knows they're quiet enough girls and I've nothing against all-girlie parties, but I do wish they weren't always so miserable and intense. You don't think they'll start burning their bras in my hall? I can't stick the smell of scorching.'

Roxanne Alder, the girl with whom I shared the attic flat, was temporarily away on a modelling job. She had left welcoming messages strung all round the place and enough food in the fridge on the landing beside the cooker to keep me for a month.

In Martha's at seven-fifteen on Monday morning, the Night Superintendent reminded me of Bert Mercer. 'Have you been away, Nurse Maitland?'

I explained myself.

'Luke? Oh—yes—I've a note about you from Miss Evans.' The Chief Nursing Officer. 'Here we are—yes—well, Staff Nurse, you'll get to Luke eventually, but as we appear to have a minor influenza epidemic on our hands, you're presently needed elsewhere.' She looked up over her glasses. 'Thirty-four staff and student nurses down since Friday. Most inconvenient as this is the holiday season. So you've been doing some more accident work in Canada?'

I hoped she did not notice the effect that had on my adrenals. 'Yes, Sister. Though technically in acute surgery, more often than not I was in reception.'

'Did their methods vary greatly from those used during your six months in our Accident Unit?'

'Apart from the terms and administrative details, there

was very little difference, Sister. Most of the surgeons and anaesthetists with whom I worked were British and had qualified here.'

'At the British taxpayer's expense,' she observed coldly. 'Presumably, that causes them no discomfort, but one wonders how comfortable they would be, were they, or their relatives, admitted as emergencies to one of the many smaller hospitals in this country chronically short of medical staff. However—to return to your immediate future. Miss Evans wants you temporarily in the Accident Unit, as first staff nurse. Both first and second are on the sick-list this morning. Sister Accidents will come on at eight and with you early—' she rootled for another note 'you will have Nurse Jones, the junior staff nurse. I'll try and catch Sister on her way in, but if I fail, when you report to her as her temporary deputy, will you explain I regret having no replacement at present for her second staff nurse, but one will be sent just as soon as a nurse with the necessary accident training can be spared from the wards.' She sat back and straightened the lace bow under her chin. 'Enjoy your break?'

'Very much, thank you, Sister.'

She was a Londoner. In the twenty years since her general training ended, she had only left Martha's to train as a midwife in Oxford. 'Provincial experience is always useful,' she said, 'but you'll be glad to be back.' Simultaneously, her tone dismissed any question of doubt in my mind, all other hospitals as second-rate, the existence of the Atlantic Ocean, and myself. It amused me, but explained why nine out of ten nurses in the outside world reacted with an instant snarl to the name Martha's, why so many Canadians had anti-English chips, and why Joss occasionally walked Martha's wards in a Benedict's tie.

The prospect of seeing him so soon, plus working with him, was such a glorious bonus that I was almost scared to dwell on it. Fortunately the problem of being temp. dep.

25

to a Sister who neither knew nor was expecting me proved life needn't be suspected of being too perfect. I had yet to meet the Sister, anywhere, who didn't detest sudden senior staff changes, and above all having to hand over to an unknown deputy. Yet even here Joss being a Benedict's man was another bonus. If Sister Accidents in two days had to cope with an unknown acting S.A.O. and myself, on past showing, God help us all.

Five years ago our old Casualty Department had been rehoused in the ground floors of the new and adjoining General Surgical and Orthopaedic Blocks and renamed Emergencies and Accidents. The twin departments remained under the overall charge of the former Sister Casualty, Miss Mackenzie. She now presided in Emergencies, which was infinitely the larger department. Every non-accident patient admitted to any of the two thousand beds came in through Emergencies. This was staffed by a posse of junior sisters, staff nurses, student nurses, medical orderlies and medic. students acting as dressers. The S.M.O. and S.S.O. had their own offices and examination rooms in the department and all the non-A.U. residents worked there on rota. The A.U. men—and Martha's had yet to appoint a woman doctor to Accidents even as anaesthetist—were the only residents in the hospital with no responsibilities outside the curved and windowless walls of the Accident Unit. And owing to the highly specialized and high-powered first aid that is modern immediate post-accident therapy, though hers was a junior sister's post, inside the A.U. Sister Accidents ruled as absolutely as any Sister Theatre in her own theatre. Only once, and after a series of mutinous murmurs from the A.U. staff had vibrated on the grapevines, had Miss Mackenzie been known to exert her superior authority. Shortly after, there had been a new Sister Accidents. The grapevines never discovered if the previous one had resigned in fury or been sacked, but the day the new girl took over, every wire in the hospital was red hot with the news that Miss Mackenzie had smiled. Miss Mackenzie was a trim, pale, white-haired Edinburgh lady and in her thirty years as a sister had never been known to suffer fatigue, hunger, emotion, or fools. She could make senior consultants dither like nervous housemen, reduce the S.M.O. and S.S.O. to apologetic medic. students. Lesser ranks became jellies or lost weight, depending on their temperaments. In the last month I spent in the A.U., I shed ten pounds. A gastric 'flu bug had caused another massive staff crisis and shot me from junior to first staff nurse overnight, and then for my final terrifying week to acting Sister, with Miss Mackenzie brooding over my every move.

On my last evening, etiquette insisted I call at her office to say goodbye. She had wished me good fortune in a voice of doom. 'Miss Evans,' she added, 'has informed me of your domestic obligations. But should your mother's welfare be to your satisfaction, and some young man not persuade you otherwise—which I fear is very possible—I hope we will see you back in your training hospital.' She almost smiled. 'You may appear but a wee-bit lassie, Nurse, but you know how to work. You managed quite well, just now.'

I had reeled to the Staff Nurses' Home where my set had revived me with cooking sherry as everything stronger had been taken to our flat for the farewell party Roxanne and I were giving that night. There were now only four of my old set left; three were junior sisters and one a staff-midwife. I liked them all, but none had been amongst my particular friends. It was through one of these, Peter Anthony, that I knew what the girls were doing. Peter I had known years. When I left he had been a senior house-physician and his last letter some time in January said he had ended all with Sue—or it could have been Carol—was uncertain about his future but thinking of trying anaes-thetics. Peter Anthony's uncertainty was one of the few

27

certainties in an uncertain world. As long as I had known him, when he ended all with the pre-Sue-Carol legion, he had spent hours flat on the floor of our living-room bleating about his uncertain future and why no one ever liked him. Roxanne and I only objected on one count. Our room was small and Peter was six three and weighed fifteen stone. When not bleating, he was good fun, being very easy-going, generous with his car, and invaluable as a chucker-out at our parties. He had never made a serious pass at either of us and only once a mild one at me when he brought me back from a rather bad party. He had turned up the following morning, a Sunday, smitten with guilt and a crashing hangover. After two pots of black coffee he said it must've been the vodka as he'd never fancied me and did I fancy him? I said sorry, no. He said that figured as he knew no one ever fancied him. He knew he was a sexual failure. He knew he would never make it in general medicine, he wasn't sure whether he should try pathology and did I know the name of the dolly with red hair and legs last night and better still her 'phone number. I had forgotten her name now, but not her keeping him off our carpet for a good two months. As I had also forgotten to answer his last letter, I wondered if anyone had told him I was coming back, or if he had left Martha's. Someone in the A.U. would know. There was always someone in every department who knew everything about everyone.

The junior staff nurse was alone in the nurses' changing-room. She had her back to me but I recognized her instantly though I had never before seen her in a staff nurse's uniform. 'You're this Jones! Hi!'

Her real name was Helen Jones, but her set had nick-named her Dolly long before they were out of the P.T.S. She had the smooth dark fringe, wide long-lashed blue eyes, chubby cheeks and dimpled chin of a Victorian china doll. When we last worked together on the same day and night shift in Albert two years ago, she had been the best junior I ever came across. I was delighted to see her and certain she was the girl whose name Joss hadn't remembered. Behind that china doll's face, Dolly Jones had a very good brain and five good 'A' Levels to prove it. Martha's only insisted on two for student nurses.

She literally fell on my neck. 'Staff, forgive the corn, but you're corn in Egypt! When I got back from my days off yesterday, heard Chalmers had gone home with a temp. Saturday night and White was ailing sick in the Home, I nearly threw a full-blown *crise de neufs* only I couldn't as we were too something busy! But, really—a girl can take so much! Morning, noon, and night— "At St Benedict's we did it this way—"' she broke off. 'Hey! You have heard the ugly news?' I nodded, smiling. 'But the whole soul-searing story? Not only Sister but also our acting S.A.O. from that place over the river? As Peter Anthony said last night, yesterday was a black day for Martha's. Our cherished A.U., the newest and most expensively equipped department in the hospital, taken over by a brace of Benedict's throw-outs. Peter said he was very sorry he'd switched to anaesthetics, though actually he's making a rather good R.A. [Resident Anaesthetist] here. Come to that,' she added without letting me say anything, 'and though it goes against the grain to admit it, our new boy knows his accident therapy. Yesterday was nightmarish. All London took to the roads and half ended up in mangled messes in here. The new boy coped as well as Stan L.' She flapped her long eyelashes. 'Wonder why Benedict's chucked him out?'

I had intended asking how long Peter had been A.U. R.A., but was too incensed on Joss's behalf to remember. 'Couldn't he have chosen? For the chance to work with Hoadley East? Even Benedict's must know Hoadley's one of the best orthopod surgeons in the world.'

'I guess so—' she did a double-take. 'How do you know this? Don't say you know Joss Desmond too! Is there a woman either side of the river who's not on first names with the man? Top of the pin-up pops is our Mr D.—and they do say as hot off the job as he is on—only for God's sake don't let Butler hear you say that as he's her private property! How do you know him?'

I was about to explain my family had lived next door to his for the first nineteen years of my life when I properly registered all she had said. I didn't believe it all, but it was a useful reminder of the efficiency of our grapevine. I said I had been at school with Ruth Desmond, his only sister, and asked about Peter.

'He came to us just after me—ten weeks back. He took a course earlier this year, then had a short spell in the General Theatre—didn't you know? He knew last night you were coming to us today. He got it from one of the Office Sisters. That's how I knew. He said he was going to ring you—didn't he?' I shook my head. 'He was fearfully pleased. Biggest erotic thrill he's had since you left from the way he was carrying on. I haven't known him so chatty since he used to haunt you in Albert—I say, did you say Ruth Desmond?'

'Yes.' Suddenly I felt much happier. Her thinking me capable of giving Peter an erotic thrill showed how much salt the rest needed. 'Why?'

'You weren't by any chance at the wedding on Saturday? You were? Oh my Gawd, Staff—don't mention it! Please! He ditched a date with Butler for it, or went off without her, or something, and the atmosphere between them first thing yesterday morning was sheer ruddy murder for the poor ruddy staff. Luckily, he made with the charm and softened her up,' she smiled, 'which didn't surprise me one little bit. Dead sexy, that man. He could soften me up any day of the week and twice on Sundays, if I weren't allergic to queues. I must say, it's going to be quite amusing having something sexy around the joint for once. Maybe I should cross the river?'

The student nurses were arriving from their breakfast. 'Maybe,' I suggested, 'we should get started? And as you know Sister's form, will you start them off?'

'Sure. Oh—by the way—how were the States?'

'United, I believe. I've been in Canada.'

She gave me one of her innocent dolly stares. 'Golly gosh, Staff, I wouldn't know the difference. I dropped geography before 'O's.' She held open the door for me. 'Sister likes us to muster in the Receiving Room. She calls it "the R.R." and the A.U. "the Unit".'

'Fair enough, I suppose.'

Dolly said meekly, 'She calls Miss Mackenzie "Sister Emergencies".'

That did shake me. 'Oh, no!' Miss Mackenzie answered with composure to 'Sister', 'Sister Casualty', or 'Miss Mackenzie'. 'Sister Emergencies' evoked a look that could fragment a diamond. 'Why hasn't someone tactfully warned Butler?'

'So who wants a shelf in a morgue fridge?'

'That bitchy?' I suddenly remembered how very little Joss had said about Butler. 'She know her stuff?'

Dolly nodded gloomily. 'She's got a gold medal. That's why Miss Evans gave her the job.'

I said slowly, 'Hospitals don't throw out their gold medals. Why on earth did she cross the river?'

'Seeing you know Joss Desmond—if he were yours would you let him off the hook without a fight? Not that he showed any inclination to put up one, yesterday. Maybe she did the right thing following him over. Maybe he'll achieve the impossible and turn this back into a happy department.'

'It isn't?'

She shook her head. 'Chalmers and Stan L. get along with Butler pretty well as they've just got to, since they work in each other's pockets. White can't stick her guts, and vice versa. She makes George Charlesworth nervous

31

—he's J.A.O. and rather sweet. Peter Anthony says he and she simply don't communicate.'

'How about you?'

She hesitated. 'I like the way she works and I like the work here. It's the atmosphere and the constant "at St. Benedict's" that makes me want to throw up. This last month the atmosphere's been so thick I think Miss Mackenzie's caught on to it. One of my set's staffing in Emergencies. She says old Mother Mack wasn't at all pleased by all the staff changes in here during Butler's first two months.'

'Who went?'

'The last R.A. didn't take up the option on his second six months—that's how Peter got here. One staff nurse and two student nurses asked Matron for transfers. One had to be put under sedation. Didn't do the A.U. any good and everyone knows it's the Sister who makes or louses up every department.'

I was trying to be detached. It wasn't easy, but I was trying. 'Accident work isn't everybody's baby but you have to get here to find that out.'

'Oh well,' said Dolly under her breath as we joined the waiting nurses, 'if you're determined to spread Christian charity, you've come to a joint that can use it.'

I suspended thought till I waited in Sister's empty office at five to eight. It was one of a row of small offices lying off one side of the narrow corridor leading from the staff exit from the Receiving Room and ending in our changing-room. I opened the large log-book on the desk and looked through the long list of yesterday's admissions. In every case the 'seen and examined on admission' column was signed 'J. R. Desmond, F.R.C.S., Acting S.A.O.'

I thought about Dolly. She enjoyed a good gossip and improving on a good story, but she was neither a liar nor a fool. I thought about Joss on Saturday. Then, simply, I didn't know what to think. I closed the book with a snap as quick steps came down the corridor. The next thing I knew was Peter Anthony lifting me up by the waist to kiss me as I was a foot shorter than himself.

'Peter, off! Down, boy!' I freed myself and dodged round the desk. 'Want to get us both slung out first thing on a Monday morning?'

He backed smiling to block the doorway as he smoothed his slightly curly and very yellow hair. It was shorter than when I had last seen him and cleared his collar by about half an inch but his sideboards were longer and thicker. I had forgotten he was so good-looking as he was one of those people I invariably forgot in their absence and was delighted to see in person. 'Hell, Cath,' he protested, 'we're alone so what better start to a Monday morning? You don't know how I've missed you! Why didn't you answer your 'phone last night? I'd have come straight round if I hadn't been on call.'

'Didn't hear the 'phone. Probably with my landlady—'
'I'll forgive you.' He lunged at me again.
'Peter, watch it! Sister's due!'

'My God, so she is! I don't know if you've been warned, but—' he glanced cautiously over his shoulder and turned puce. 'Oh, sorry—want to come in?' He stepped aside and my heart seemed to lurch with joy. Joss came in slowly, wearing a clean long white coat, dark suit, Benedict's tie and a polite expression. 'Good morning,' he said, 'I'm waiting for Sister.'

Peter waved vaguely. 'You won't know each other. Mr Desmond from St Benedict's, our temp. S.A.O., Staff Nurse Maitland back home from the colonies.'

Sister had arrived, so, correctly, Joss ignored me and smiled at her. ' 'Morning, Sister!'

I was not too happy about his tie, but in any circumstances in a British hospital the safest way to play it is to stick to etiquette. I did the same. When Miss Butler had finished apologizing for delaying Joss's breakfast, I wished her a good morning as if the two men were invisible. She did not bother to answer or even look my way. 'Do you want Mr Desmond or myself, Dr Anthony?'

Joss looked at the floor and Peter as if he had been caught having a fix at the Dangerous Drug Cupboard. 'Er—neither, Sister, thanks. Just—er—collecting some notes from my office to read over breakfast.' He vanished down the corridor.

Naomi Butler was about twenty-seven. She was tallish and very slim, with light brown hair and a delicate-featured face that was much too pale. She looked to me not just grossly over-tired but ill. I wondered if she had an anaemia problem, and then as I knew I had never seen her before, why something about her seemed familiar. I had plenty of time to wonder, as she was still ignoring me and explaining why she had sent a message asking Joss to call in on his way to breakfast. 'There appears to be some industrial injuries query about the man Francis Albert Ayer we admitted to Intensive Care last evening and I thought you'd prefer to sort it out quietly before we're officially opened as you used to in St Benedict's—' she paused, frowning, as Dolly arrived. 'Well, Staff?'

'Excuse me, Sister, but a mechanic from Repairs and Works is here and would like to see you about the oxygen piping in the Shock Room.'

Joss said, 'I can wait, Sister.'

'If you wouldn't mind?' Her smile was very attractive. It disappeared when she finally turned to me. 'Staff Nurse Maitland?'

'Yes, Sister. The Night Superintendent—'

'I've seen her. I'll deal with you, directly. Wait.' She went off with Dolly.

Joss and I looked at each other. And I smiled. 'I didn't expect this, Joss.'

He didn't smile. 'Quite a turn-up for the book. Tell me

34

something, Cathy—' he took a deep breath. 'How much accident time have you actually had on this side of the Atlantic?'

I had not expected the lunatic, the lover, or the poet in the A.U. at this hour on a Monday, but nor had I expected this. I answered his question then added what I had said to Night Super.

'Uh-huh,' he grunted.

'Have a good drive back?'

'Yep. Thanks. Get to your digs all right?'

'Fine, thanks. Just fine.' He saw my glance at his tie, so I smiled again. 'I didn't realize you always wore your battle colours.'

He glanced downwards. 'I don't.'

The silence was stifling. I remembered he hadn't had breakfast. 'Busy night?'

'Not particularly.'

'From the log, yesterday seems to have been night-marish.'

'Just the usual fine summer Sunday holocaust.' He looked at me through his lashes. 'One doesn't expect to play ring o' roses on the job. Not that one's anything against the game—when one's nothing better to do.'

For a few seconds I was too angry to answer and half my anger was directed at myself. He wasn't the first man to regret Saturday night on Monday morning, but he was the first I had taken seriously. 'Can't say it's ever really sent me. How's Stan Lawson this morning? I haven't heard.'

He said very gravely, 'Not too well, I'm afraid. This seems a very nasty bug.'

'Very nasty,' I agreed as Sister came back.

Chapter Three

'And another police call coming your way, Staff.' The Head Porter rustled some notes at his end of the line. 'One male, one female. Youngish. Minor lacerations, bruises, shock. Driver and front seat passenger, in private car A. Head on, private car B—not going too fast, am I?'

'Just getting that, thanks, Mr Jarvis.' I wrote swiftly on the huge memo pad on the standing desk fixed to the wall at the far end of the Receiving Room. The remainder of the wall was occupied by a line of scrubbing-up sinks.

The three telephones on the desk were red, yellow and green. Set above and on either side of every door in the department were three similarly coloured bulbs. All incoming calls were announced by flashing lights and the only bell ever sounded was the fire alarm. The red was only used to herald admissions; yellow, for outside calls coming through the main switchboard; green, was the inter-hospital line. There was a red telephone in every room and office in the A.U., including our changing-room.

'Car B, Mr Jarvis?'

'Haven't got 'em out yet. Two involved and up front. Both unconscious, seemly, and in a right mess. One male, one female. Small car, no belts visible. They've got the firemen out.'

'Car A wearing belts, I take it?'

'That's right. Some,' he added laconically, 'never learn, do they? Should be here in about ten minutes.'

Sister glanced through my notes then passed them to Joss. There was a temporary lull on and they were in Cubicle 1 with the four final year medic. students working as accident dressers for that week. The only girl medic. asked, 'Why the fire brigade, Mr Desmond?'

'They've the right type of tin-openers for this type of job.' As the room was empty of patients, all the cubicle curtains were drawn back. Joss looked the five accident tables over. '4 and 5 for these two, Sister? Right. Eccles—' he nodded at one student, '5 with Mr Palmer. [The houseman.] Huntly, 4 with Mr Charlesworth. Miss—er—'

'Dawson,' said Sister before the girl could open her mouth.

'Thanks.' He told the girl to shadow Dr Anthony and the final student to stick by him. 'MacDonald, isn't it?'

'That's right,' echoed Sister and the student together.

The A.U. trained staff always worked in pairs that were arranged by Sister at the start of each day. At present, Sister was paired with Joss, Dolly with Mr Charlesworth, Nurse Henty, the senior student nurse, with Mr Palmer, and Nurse Fisher, a third-year with more A.U. time than all the other student nurses with the exception of Henty, was with Peter. The most junior houseman, Mr Geddes, was in our plaster theatre for the day, and officially assisted by Mr Kovac, the plaster technician. Mr Kovac, a middle-aged and highly competent Pole, had run the plaster theatre since the A.U. opened. He was a good and tactful teacher.

As necessary the pairs became a team of four, six, or eight, working simultaneously on the same patient. When possible, 1 and 2 were reserved for the most injured, being technically the senior cubicles, but they were all identically equipped and had enough floor space for a team of ten to work, uncramped. Each had its own anaesthetic machine, sucker and respirator, piped oxygen supply, trolleys set with sealed sterile dressing and instrument packs for anything from removing a splinter to the amputation of a limb. The trolleys with metal stands painted red instead of the ubiquitous white held the settings for emergency tracheotomy and cardiac arrest.

The tables looked rather like operating tables but were far more comfortable to lie on. A battery of buttons raised or lowered transfusion and drip stands, altered any part or the whole table to any position wanted. The previous Sister Accidents said the only thing her tables could not do was walk, but give the designers time and they would get that taped. In the rare temporary lull on a Monday morning, she had always demonstrated their uses to the new medic. students starting their weekly rota. I had not yet seen Miss Butler address a direct word to any of them. She gave the impression of regarding them as a necessary evil she was prepared to suffer but under no circumstances enjoy. She wasn't unique in that, nor in the cold glances she had given Miss Dawson's heels and hemline when she first appeared. I could think without difficulty of a dozen sisters with the same reaction. The student girl's hemline was now hidden by her gown and from the way she was standing, the sooner she could get her feet into flatties the happier she'd be.

My job for the morning was 'lights and messages'. 'You won't be any use to me till you've had a refresher,' Sister's tone dismissed my Canadian job as a sinecure best forgotten. 'A year off's a long time.'

The A.U. was officially open from 8 a.m. to 10 p.m. seven days a week and when closed could open at any hour for major emergencies, minor accidents at night being dealt with in Emergencies. The large night staff there always included at least one staff nurse with accident training. When necessary she worked in the

38

A.U. at night with other nurses from Emergencies, but as Martha's had no shift system for residents, with the A.U. men. These had a weekly rota which gave them—on paper—every other night off-call, one weekly half-day, one free evening, and every other weekend off. The 'week-end' began at noon on Saturday and ended at midnight on Sunday. I could remember the one week when Stan Lawson, as J.A.O., had all his official time off, on time. It had happened in my first month and was still an unbeaten record when I left.

Long before the A.U. first opened, time and motion experts worked out in detail the nurses' shifts. The result was impressive. Every night at ten, all we had to do was hand over to the Emergencies girls and go home. The time and motion experts had done their homework, but they had never worked in an A.U., as hospitals with such units were still rare and hadn't existed when most of them qualified, or trained. It was hard enough to hand over a ward on time when a patient has just had a coronary, or is having a major haemorrhage. It was impossible to remember the clock, much less hand over, when attending to a human being soaked in blood, grime, oil, and with the ends of broken bones visible through a business suit, or dance dress.

Miss Evans understood this. She insisted the student nurses work only their allotted shifts, but left Sister Accidents free to arrange the hours of her staff nurses and herself, providing we somehow got the right number of hours off every week. But the only fixed free time on which we could depend were our two weekly days off. The uncertainty obviously affected our social lives and this was why Miss Evans still refused to appoint any married nurse as Sister Accidents. Stan Lawson was the only married S.A.O. we had so far had, but as his wife worked in the hospital and they had a hospital flat just across the road, in their case it was working out pretty well. Any married man with a family living out was unlikely to have more than three nights a month at home. The tiny hospital flats, originally for bachelors, were now rented to married staff without children. This was another of the many reasons why the S.A.O.'s job appealed only to that handful of individualists.

The red light flashed again. As I reached for the red 'phone, Sister called down the room, 'Lights, Nurse!'

Again, Mr Jarvis: 'Elderly gent. for you, Staff. Seventy-odd. Query fractured left femur. Shock. Stepped in front of a double-decker without looking—bit hard of hearing, I shouldn't wonder. On his way in—hold it, Staff! And another! Little lad. Query greenstick fracture right forearm, minor lacerations, shock. Come off his bike —day off for half-term, I reckon. Parents not yet contacted—got that?'

'Nearly.' The occupants of car A were being wheeled in on low accident stretcher-trolleys. I asked if he knew more of car B?

'Seems they're having a bit of trouble still. The roof's caved down like a sardine tin that's been stamped on, they say.' He rang off and I winced.

The small boy, Mark Alan Langley, arrived before the elderly man, a Mr William Henry Pears. Mark was eight, fair, skinny, and it was his first visit to a hospital. Though without his parents and surrounded by masked and gowned strangers, he was as sensible and co-operative as the most intelligent adult. But unlike an adult on finding himself a patient for the first time, Mark was totally unimpressed by all he saw.

Mr Palmer and Nurse Henty were attending to him. Joss had seen him and ordered his treatment on admission, as he did for every patient, then returned to Mr Pears in C2. He took another look at Mark as the technician was adjusting the angle of the portable X-ray machine. The Langley parents had been contacted, 'phoned their consent for treatment and were on their way up. 'Comfortable, Mark?' asked Joss.

Mark said he was O.K. but unless they were all right nuts he didn't see how the bloke could get a picture of his arm from underneath the bed thing. 'This metal'll cut out the rays.'

'It won't.' Joss explained the bed and mattress were specially constructed to let the rays pass through. He used 'constructed', not 'made'.

Mark remained unimpressed. 'Colour pictures?'

The technician apologized. 'No.'

'Am I on closed-circuit t.v.? Don't you even have closed-circuit t.v.?'

'I'm afraid not,' said Joss.

'I say,' said Mark, 'this is a rather grotty old hospital, isn't it?'

Mr Palmer drawled apologetically, 'We have been going six hundred years.'

'Cor, that's older than my grandad! No wonder it's creaky.'

Dolly was washing at the sink next to the desk when Sister paused by me. 'Nurse Maitland, will you inform me directly the Langleys arrive, but put them in the relatives' rest-room and offer them tea.'

Dolly waited till Sister moved away. 'What does she think you are? A first-year?'

'Maybe Benedict's first-years don't answer 'phones and make the tea.'

She pulled a face behind her mask. 'Maybe Benedict's haven't sent us the rightest little megalomaniac in the business.'

A few minutes later, Mr Palmer re-scrubbed beside me. He was a tallish, willowy young man with a very trendy hair-cut and a languid air. He was nearly as dark as Joss but had blue not brown eyes. I had seen him around at parties as a student, but this was the first time we had

41

worked together. 'Great place this for crushing the ego into the ground,' he murmured behind his mask. 'Do you suppose that revoltingly erudite little monster's mama was once a Miss Butler?'

I caught his eye. Joss was only a yard away. 'I've no more details yet, Mr Palmer, as Mark's parents haven't arrived.' He glanced round and then winked at me without saying more.

Peter was next to use that sink. 'How much longer are they going to be getting those poor sods out of car B?'

I told him what Mr Jarvis had said and he winced. 'How are the Gamlins?' The couple in Car A.

'Desmond says she can go home once she's rested-up, and he shouldn't be warded more than overnight.'

I smiled voluntarily. 'That's something.'

His eyes smiled over his mask. 'I'm glad you're with us. Every time this morning I've felt the gods have it in for me I've looked at you and changed my mind. Know what I mean?'

I knew exactly. Being a small blonde with curves, if under-developed, in the right places, I had long come to terms with the fact that to most men I wasn't a sex symbol, I was a teddy-bear substitute. I got cuddled, but seldom embraced. Joss on Saturday night had been a new experience for me as well as one I now wanted to forget as fast I could—if I could. Angry as he had made me, seeing him all morning wasn't making things easier.

He had moved to the sink beside Peter's. Soaping his hands and arms, he looked my way as casually as Stan Lawson or any other S.A.O. would have done. 'Taking them the hell of a time getting that car open. Much longer and the poor bastards'll come in as B.I.D.s.' Brought In Dead.

Peter said he was thinking that. 'Anyone with them?'

'Mr Jarvis hasn't said, but presumably they've got some medic. there as our Crash Team hasn't been called out.'

Sister caught my eye and beckoned. 'Staff, I wouldn't have thought it necessary to say this to a nurse of your seniority, but possibly you've acquired some different professional standards in the past year. In future, please remember, I do not like my staff to gossip on-duty.'

She was Sister, so I apologized meekly, though I thought she was mistaken. I thought that again in the next temporary lull. Car B was now on everyone's mind. The men and medic. students were standing around or sitting on high stools, staring into space. The nurses were silently dealing with the clearing, checking and re-stocking that went on constantly between cases. I thought the silence unhealthy. Formerly, here even more than in the theatres, when patientless, the staff had used casual, crazy, even heated discussions, as a safety-valve. The whole staff, as all the nurses were senior students, since only third and fourth years worked in the A.U. The present atmosphere reminded me of my first ward ex-P.T.S. and how much my set as well as myself had resented being treated by our nursing and medical seniors as moronic machines the year after we'd grown accustomed to being accepted as intelligent young adults in our sixth forms. At the end of that year Miss Evans had become our first C.N.O., instead of Matron. She was still in her thirties. Her revolutionary ideas on the treatment of student nurses had horrified many, but not all, our older sisters, but inside of two years had cut the Martha's drop-out rate amongst student nurses by twenty per cent. Looking around it struck me as time St Benedict's had a Miss Evans, and then I noticed Joss surveying the room in much the same way as myself.

Mr Palmer had been strolling round aimlessly. He stopped to watch some adjustments Peter was making to the anaesthetic machine in C1 and obviously absently, after fiddling with a pair of scissors lying on a shelf by his hand, put them in his pocket. Sister rounded on him as if he had been caught shop-lifting. 'Mr Palmer, those scissors you're secreting happen to be my private property!'

It was a very little thing. In any department the wrong scissors got picked up by the wrong owners a dozen times a day. But as everyone was on edge, it united the home staff into an outraged band of brothers and sisters. Mr Palmer's reactions enhanced the unity.

'Sister, I'm stricken with remorse—but stricken!' Bowing affectedly, he returned her scissors at arms' length. 'Pray accept my most humble—nay—profound apologies and assurances that to take your personal property is the last thing I would ever desire to do. How can I make amends?'

Joss said, 'Just ask Mr Jarvis for a couple of sacks, nip down to the basement for some ashes from the boiler-house, get off those shoes and get started for Canterbury. It's only sixty odd miles.'

Sister had looked ready to hit Mr Palmer, but as Joss had spoken, she smiled weakly. The staff had its first, and only, communal laugh of the morning.

The red light jerked every head towards me. I shook mine as Mr Jarvis dictated: 'Male, 21, burns to face, head, arms. Motor mechanic. Minor explosion in garage work-shop. No others involved.'

The red light continued to flash with the monotony of traffic signals. At last: 'Got 'em out, Staff. Car B. Both on their way—'

'Thank God for that, Mr Jarvis.'

'That's as maybe, Staff. Ready?'

I braced myself. Mr Jarvis was an experienced and humane man. 'Sure.'

The police had discovered the couple's names and address. They were a Mr and Mrs Yates and in their forties. Mr Yates had visible multiple injuries to his head, chest and both legs. Mrs Yates' visible injuries were worse.

44

'Nasty,' added Mr Jarvis.

'God,' I muttered, 'yes.'

Joss grimaced as he read my notes over Sister's shoulder. He gave them to the medic. students. 'Take a look so you'll know what to expect. And remember what I told you earlier. No one'll mind if you feel queasy, providing you get yourselves out before you pass out. No bloody heroics, please.' He turned to Sister. 'We'll start with four on each.'

Sister nodded. 'Nurse Maitland, as I'll probably be held up, will you see Mrs Gamlin gets a lunch-tray in the S.R. [Shock Room] and make her some fresh tea.'

'Yes, Sister.'

Dolly and Henty exchanged mutinous glances. I was tempted to mutiny with them, but I had to see Sister's angle, now, if I hadn't earlier. I had never worked in the present accident team. For any team of any nature to work well takes regular practice together as well as skill. Practice takes time; there was none to spare in the present situation. It was an A.U. maxim that the longer a dangerously injured patient took to reach us, the less time there was to save his or her life. Once the Yates's arrived and Joss decided what had to be done, and done first, for them, the team had to know without more talk, not only their own but everyone else's job.

In these cases, the S.A.O. never had more than minutes for his decisions. There was no time for consulting the opinions of pundits, taking X-rays, or pathological tests. In time the last two would be taken probably by the dozen, providing the S.A.O. had correctly judged which was the most serious injury or clinical condition requiring the most immediate treatment. A snap decision would have been difficult enough when examining an unknown patient in a clean nightgown in a ward bed for the first time. Accident victims were generally fully dressed, but no matter how they started out, no one stays clean after being involved in a bad road smash. The diagnosis of visible injuries could be complicated by clotted blood and road dirt, but brain and internal damage did not always show up at once in a patient already in coma from shock. The last Sister Accidents once said that in her view to be a good S.A.O. took experience, skill and guts in equal parts.

Joss, Sister, Peter, the pathologist on A.U. call for the day, went out to meet the ambulance, and up into it when it arrived. It seemed a long time before the stretcher trolleys were wheeled in. It was less than five minutes.

The green flashed. 'S.S.O.,' announced Mr Roth's rather harsh voice. 'Mr Desmond free? Oh—? Right. I'll ring back, later. What's that—message? No. Purely domestic issue. Can wait.'

The pale green and opaque fibre glass curtains were closed round C1 and on either side of C2. Mrs Yates was in 1. She had been in there about twenty minutes when Miss Dawson came through the curtains and slowly towards me. She was an attractive girl with a naturally high colour and auburn hair. Her face was pale green before she began to sway.

'Here.' 5 was empty. I switched shut the curtains with one hand, pushed her onto the table with the other. 'Stretch out, love, or you'll pass out.' I pressed the button that raised her feet above her head. 'Stay put whilst I answer that yellow. I'll be back.'

Her face was damp and she closed her eyes. 'Thanks.'

'Is the S.A.O. available to take an outside call, Staff? He's not—oh, don't tell me!' The switchboard girl sighed. 'I've got a caller hanging on that's not going to like this. A Mr Hall. Grandad of a kid called Mark Alan Langley.'

'He doesn't want us, he wants Charity. We sent him up there over an hour ago.'

'Staff, do you mind? I'd a word with Mr Jarvis soon as Mr Hall was on the line and put him onto Sister Charity.

46

And a right barny they had! I only got the finish—he's going to be writing his M.P., the Health Minister, the Prime Minister—the lot! Don't ask me why, nor why he says he insists on getting an official report for his record—don't ask me what record. Sounds dead spare, he does, and he's not going to like this wait! Shall I put him on to you?'

I damned Sister Charity, mentally. Her tactlessness with relatives was only beaten by her excellence at nursing sick children. 'Sure. See what I can do.'

'And the best of British to you, mate,' she said in one voice, and in another, 'The Staff Nurse in the Accident Unit is on the line to you now, sir.'

Mr Hall had an educated voice and was in a flaming temper that was probably two-thirds delayed-action anxiety. He had had, he said, as much nonsense as he could stand from domineering women and he did not propose to take any more from me. He was not asking for the moon, he was merely asking for the simple courtesy that was incidentally his right as a tax-payer. 'Whom do you imagine pays your salary, young woman? My fellow tax-paying citizens and myself! Be good enough to ask the surgeon who attended my grandson, Mark Langley, on admission, to spare me three minutes of his time. I'll wait.'

I watched the drawn curtains round 1 and 2. He sounded the type to bombard Miss Evans, the Dean, and the Editor of *The Times* with irate letters, though on what grounds only God and Sister Charity knew. In these circumstances, that should not do Joss and Sister any harm, but as anyone with any experience of hospital life would understand, unfairly, it would not do them any good. Sister Charity was in a different situation, being a long-established law unto herself. Every paediatrician in Martha's knew she was tactless with relatives, but would go to the stake rather than lose her nursing talents.

47

Then I remembered Butler's remark about different professional standards and an elderly Canadian nurse with whom I had worked. On similar occasions, she'd mutter to herself, 'You want the truth, huh? Buster, you will surely get a load of it!' Her technique worked superbly on English-Canadians, Scots-Canadians, French-Canadians, British-British.

And Mr Hall.

'Is that so? Dear, dear, dear! How most distressing! Naturally, you can't consider disturbing the surgeon's concentration—Mr Desmond, did you say? When would you suggest I call him back? Three-thirty? Before the evening rush-hour starts? I quite understand—thank you —if you would tell him to expect my call then? You will? Most obliged—may I ask your name? Ah! Tell me, Staff Nurse Maitland, did you by any chance see my grandson when he was admitted to your department? Very shaken, I've no doubt, without his parents—I beg your pardon— oh!' His voice was now oozing pride. 'Well, well! I'm delighted to hear he behaved himself. He's not a bad little fellow, really, but being my only grandchild—yes, I thought you'd understand. Good day to you!'

Miss Dawson had lowered her feet and was sitting up. 'Someone giving you his life's history?'

I nodded and wrote a note telling Joss to expect the call and why, then pinned it to the baize board above the desk. I took her pulse. 'Your colour's better but I shouldn't go back yet.'

She shuddered. 'Must I? At all?' She read the answer in my expression. 'Or switch subjects?'

I nodded again to save our voices disturbing the others and beckoned her to follow me into the Shock Room. The fourth-year student nurse working in there was try-ing an assortment of slippers on a youth who had cracked his left tibia falling off his scooter and was waiting for his plaster to dry before going home. Our Shock Room was in

48

actual fact less dramatic than it sounded, being where our patients rested until going home. The only other patient there now was Mrs Gamlin. She was asleep behind drawn curtains.

Miss Dawson took a look round them, then came and sat on a stool by the standing desk that was a twin with the one in the Receiving Room. 'I can't believe they were in the same accident.'

'The Gamlins' car was much bigger and heavier—and they had on belts.'

'That's what Mr Desmond said. He's good, isn't he?'

'I've only worked with him this morning, but I've heard he is.'

'He must be or Hoadley East wouldn't have shoved him in over our own men's heads—and even the orthopod boys admit Desmond knows his orthopaedics. But that woman—' She was shuddering again. 'Did you see what she looks like? No hair—no face—she didn't even look human. I was all right, till I suddenly realized she was a woman—I don't know why that did it?'

I said, 'There but for the Grace of God . . .' I got her some tea from the urn. 'This is a bit stewed. I'll make fresh soon, if you'd like to wait.'

'This is bliss, thanks.' She looked at the Martha's badge on my apron bib. 'How long've you been a staff nurse?'

I had to think. 'It's over two years since I finished midder.'

'That long! Why on earth are you making the tea and answering the 'phone?'

'Someone has to.' The green was on. 'Accident Unit. Staff Nurse Maitland speaking.'

'Canteen here, Staff,' said an aggrieved female voice. 'That lunch you ordered for a patient. It's ready, but you'll have to send someone to fetch it. Lunches have started. We're much too busy to run your errands.'

'We'll collect it, thanks.' I rang off and asked Miss

Dawson if she would get the tray. 'Just take off that gown and mask. I'll explain to Sister, later.'

'Thanks,' she said, 'thanks a lot.' Then she said, 'Staff, does one get used to this?' I shook my head. 'That why Sister looks so ill? Being at it all the time?' She looked upwards as I suddenly reached for the green 'phone. 'What's happened to that green? It's gone red and it's not flashing.'

The nurse across the room caught my eye. I said, 'Yes, Sister,' rang off, and took Miss Dawson into the corridor. I closed the door, picked up the green receiver on the wall shelf. 'Lodge, please. Mr Jarvis? Accident Unit, Nurse Maitland. Morgue trolley, please. Yes. Mrs Yates.'

Miss Dawson leant against the wall. 'I—I suppose you still want that tray?'

'Please.'

In the Receiving Room, Joss was washing at the sink by the desk. We exchanged bleak glances. I told him the trolley was coming.

'Thanks, Staff,' he said mechanically, and went on soaping his hands and arms to above the elbows.

Chapter Four

By Thursday in that week the 'flu epidemic in south-east England was making front-page headlines; the London hospitals were only admitting emergencies to medical beds; Florence and Stephen, our sick-staff wards, had overspilled into the Private Wing; our S.M.O., Dr Gray, was daily risking violent injury from his juniors by his reiteration that the worst was yet to come; and I was still on 'lights and messages'.

There were some minor changes in the A.U. One of the medics., Mr Eccles, and a fourth-year student nurse had caught 'flu. The latter had been replaced by a girl in Henty's set who only finished her A.U. time last month. Her name was Rosalind Roberts and the Office appointed her to Henty's job, and moved Henty and Dolly up to acting third and second staff nurse. This seemed to please Sister, even if it did not stop her brooding over us like a short-tempered if highly efficient ghost, or encourage her to take more than a fraction of her official daily off-duty

Having worked with a few other sisters equally determined to work themselves into the ground, though I enjoyed the attitude no more than most senior staff nurses, it only worried me now as it looked to me as if that was precisely what Butler was going to do. Neither Dolly nor

Peter agreed. Dolly said she couldn't recall Sister looking anything but ready for a shelf in a morgue fridge. 'She always hung around when Chalmers and White were on.'

'As much as now?'

'Not quite—but she hadn't her very own dashing white surgeon running the shop then. Can't say I blame her.' She flapped her china-doll eyelashes. 'I fancy Sister's D.W.S.'

'I thought you didn't fancy queues?'

'So where does it say a girl can't change her mind?'

Peter was convinced all that ailed Sister could be put right with a few shots of iron. 'Half the women in England are only over-tired because they're short of iron.' He reached out a hand and hitched down my lower eyelids. 'You could use some, Cath.'

We were in the canteen just then. My feet were hurting after standing around all morning watching others working under pressure and my temper was unimproved by the chat Joss was having with a pale, willowy brunette physiotherapist in the coffee queue. She was of the same physical type as Miss Butler and I suddenly realized why the latter had struck me as familiar when we first met. All the girls Joss had brought home in the past could also have been painted by Burne-Jones.

'Don't maul, Pete! I loathe it!'

He looked ready to burst into tears. He had had a bad morning. Sister had snapped at him for breaking a large glass funnel, his mother had written him a stern postcard for forgetting his father's birthday and he had had a letter from his bank manager about his overdraft. He insisted he hadn't meant to maul as he knew no one liked being mauled by him and if I was going to be like that he'd just settle for the fact he hadn't a friend in the world. He glowered at Joss's back. 'Why do some chaps have it made? What's he got that I haven't—as if I didn't know?'

'Well, if you fancy Butler—?'

52

That cheered him. 'Rather settle for my bank manager. What am I going to say to the sod, Cath?'

We drafted a placating letter for the rest of our break. When we left, Joss and the physio were at a table by the door. He didn't turn his head. Nor did I, but I've always had excellent sideways vision.

Had Joss and I only met again in Martha's, he would have been the obvious, and first, person I'd have asked about Butler's health. Last Saturday had altered our relationship more than I would have believed possible until it happened. Previously, after some other man and I stopped dating each other, we had always stayed on amicable terms, and I had never known any of those dates as long, and well, as I knew Joss. It took me a couple of days to realize that was the basic problem. Making a fool of oneself to a semi-stranger mattered only as long as one remembered the stranger's name—if it mattered at all. But who enjoys looking a fool to a life-long friend, or easily forgives that friend for witnessing the folly? Yet oddly, and disturbingly, when watching Joss in the A.U., it never once occurred to me to think of him as Ruth's brother. I did frequently wonder if I had dreamed up Saturday night.

Thursday was invariably the quietest day of the A.U. week and that one was typical. I was off from two to five; Sister, officially, from five-thirty. When Miss Mackenzie appeared in the Receiving Room just after eight, Henty and I were alone. Sister was still in her office working on the day's notes with Joss. It being a hospital rule that all accident notes had to be entered in full in the A.U. log on the day, or night, on which they were made. After any rush of admissions, this could literally take hours and needed the S.A.O.'s co-operation owing to the complicated treatments given and the fact that his signature stood against each entry. If the S.A.O. was taking his rare time off, the J.A.O. acted for him, just as her deputy was permitted to do for Sister. I had not yet been allowed to write even the date in our log.

Henty was mending gowns and I was tidying the blank forms filing cabinet by the X-ray screens. Miss Mackenzie's advent made Henty leap off her high stool and I shut the metal filing drawer so fast it nearly took off my fingers. 'Good evening, Sister. Can I help you?'

Miss Mackenzie's grey eyes X-rayed the room, Henty and myself. 'Good evening, Staff. Are you on, or is Sister still here?' And when I explained, 'I will not disturb Miss Butler as she's busy. Kindly ask her to step into my office on her way off.' She had another look round. 'Very quiet, just now.'

'Yes, Sister. No admissions for an hour.'

'Thursday,' she said. 'Low pay packets. And whilst that is regrettable, there's no doubt in my mind the situation had saved many a life. I'll see myself out. Thank you, Staff.'

'Thank you, Sister.'

Henty and I stared at each other in silence until the airtight doors sealed themselves.

'Staff, why didn't she just pick up a 'phone?'

I did not answer at once. Henty was a quiet, trim, likeable girl and fast worker, but I didn't yet know her well enough to know if she could keep her mouth shut. 'Maybe she was just passing.'

Henty blinked thoughtfully through her steel-rimmed granny glasses. 'Do you think Sister's getting the bug?'

'I've wondered that, but as the invasion's so short, I don't think she can be. She certainly looks very tired.'

She picked up her sewing. 'She has for the last month. Could Miss Mackenzie have noticed?'

'Very little Miss Mackenzie doesn't notice.'

We exchanged another meaning stare. As she was obviously wondering how much she could trust me, she tested the ice again. 'I suppose all Sister Accidents do a lot of overtime.'

'Occupational hazard in their job.' I glanced at the wall clock. Sister objected strongly to being interrupted for non-essential reasons when writing up the log, but if she took Miss Mackenzie's visitation as that, I didn't and nor did Henty. I asked her to watch the lights whilst I went along to Sister's office.

'Hold it, Staff, hold it!' Mr Palmer swept in beaming with the eagerness of the bearer of bad news. 'My dears— my very dears—lamentable tidings! Our Stanley has right lobar pneumonia. The physicians are in a positive tiz-woz! They've got him in a tent—giving him the whole works!'

'Oh no!' Henty and I exchanged 'that's why' glances as we spoke together. 'How utterly miserable!'

'I'm very sorry to hear this, Dave.' Joss had come in, unnoticed. 'Where've they got him?'

'Stephen Small Ward One. The S.M.O.'s just said he won't be back inside of a month. And guess what else our own dear Cassandra said—'

I left them to it and went along to Sister. She was still writing at her desk, but with her head propped on her left hand as if the weight was too much for her neck. She took both my items of news with a weary sigh. 'This seems a particularly virulent virus.'

'It caused a lot of bad chests in Canada.'

'Did you get it, Staff? Not that that'll prevent your getting it again. Pity about Mr Lawson, but with anti-biotic therapy he should soon clear up. I only hope Mr Desmond keeps healthy for us.'

'Yes.' She looked so ghastly that I added, 'Sister, forgive me, but are you feeling all right? You look rather tired.'

She smiled at me for the first time. 'I'm always this colour without make-up. My grandmother used to say I should eat more carrots. She pinned her faith in the human race on carrots. Fed me so many, I now can't look at 'em.'

I had never known her so human. I was almost sorry. If I was going to start liking her, my life in the A.U.

was going to become even more complicated than it was already. Peter underlined this when he drove me home that night, being off-call. He nearly hit a bus when I suggested Butler might be human underneath.

'Scrub that! The woman's impossible! God alone knows why Joss Desmond fancies her.'

'He's fancied highly strung neuros since he was in hot pants at prep school.'

'How do you know that?'

I pretended I had forgotten to tell him. 'Didn't Dolly Jones tell you I was at school with Ruth Desmond?'

He shook his head, gloomily. 'She's not on speaking terms with me now as I'm a chum of old George. He and Dolly've had another of their out-fallings.'

'Dolly and George Charlesworth? A pair? Since when?'

'Last few months. Haven't you noticed they've been at each other's throats all week?'

'No.' I was surprised and intrigued. 'Are they serious?'

'Don't know that she is. Poor old George has got it badly. He's dead glum now. He says Dolly fancies Joss Desmond. Seems every woman in Martha's fancies the guy. Do you?'

'I have this anti-thing to crowds.'

He laughed and drew up outside my landlady's house. 'I didn't think you would. For starters, you couldn't push him around. You've never gone for guys you can't push around—or with dark hair.' He smoothed his blond hair smugly. 'It's the Nordic charm that sends you. Going to ask me up for coffee?'

'If you want some and you make it.'

He got out of the car. 'Know what sends me about you? The gracious warmth of your invitations.'

I smiled peevishly. 'Come off it, Pete! You know I make lousy coffee and Roxanne's still away making a telly commercial somewhere in the Italian Alps.'

My landlady was in the hall. She had always liked Peter

and greeted him as if he were back from Canada. Over the coffee he made very well I asked why he had not contacted Roxanne whilst I was away.

'With my overdraft?'

'I'll bet Roxanne's is bigger. She earns a lot when she's working, but she isn't always in work.'

'She seems to do all right without.' He got off the sofa for a closer look at the full length photo on the bookshelf of Roxanne modelling a lace trouser suit. In common with most of the men who were my friends he had never been able to believe Roxanne's highly decorative exterior hid an ardent and very hard-working career girl. 'Why hasn't she yet managed to land one of the well-heeled legion she runs around with?'

'She doesn't want to. She likes working.'

'I suppose being a champagne girlie is working—of a sort.'

'Peter,' I said, 'don't be bitchy.'

He turned, smiling. 'I just hate the idle rich. Any more coffee in that pot?'

I investigated. 'Sorry, no. Be an angel and make some more.'

He picked up the pot, then stood looking down at me, reflectively. 'Why do I let you push me around?'

'Because you and I, lovey, have a beautiful relationship.'

There was a new and very serious expression on his face. 'I can think of worse,' he said shortly, and went out to make the coffee on the cooker on the landing. I wondered absently what was on his mind, then remembered what he had said about Joss. I was in a very bad temper when he got back, but as he had relapsed into one of his 'the gods have it in for me' moods, our mutual gloom was downright companionable.

Normally, my gloom wore off overnight. Not that night. When I joined the other living-out day staff nurses waiting at the dais end of the dining-room for Night Super to read the day register in the morning, I decided leaving Canada had been the greatest mistake of my life.

Dolly Jones squeezed in beside me a minute before one of the Night Sisters arrived instead of the Super. 'Think the old girl's got the bug?' she murmured without moving her lips.

I shrugged in answer as the Night Sister was looking directly at us. 'Good morning, Nurses. As the Night Superintendant had been unavoidably detained, I'll start for her. Nurse A. L. Adams . . .'

The ward changes came after the register. The Night Sister closed the book and produced a list. 'Several changes today, Nurses. Departments first. Emergencies and Accidents. Nurse J. Smithers from Emergencies to the Accident Unit as extra fourth-year nurse. Nurse Donkin from Mark Ward to the Accident Unit as extra third-year nurse.' She looked up and at me. 'Staff Nurse Maitland, the Night Superintendent will ring you directly she is free. In the meantime will you carry on as usual with the early routine. You will find the Accident Unit already open. Now—Ear, Nose and Throat Department, Nurse M. Francis . . . .'

Dolly's eyes were closed. 'Please God, please God *not* another school bus. I can take most things,' she muttered, 'but not mangled kids.'

My stomach heaved. 'Too early.'

She breathed out. 'So it is. Forgot.'

Henty joined us as we left the dining-room. 'There was nothing about a train crash on the seven o'clock news.'

'Whatever it is,' gasped Dolly as we shot towards the A.U. 'it has to be big. Another eighteen down with the bug this morning, but we've got two extras. I'll bet we find every cubicle occupied.'

Neither Henty nor I took her up. If we had, Dolly would have lost. Our Receiving Room was empty, though looking as if someone had let off a bomb in it. The Emergencies night staff were grey with fatigue and the empty vacolitres of blood waiting to be returned to the Path. Lab. needed a stretcher-trolley instead of the usual basket.

'Sorry abut the mess, Maitland.' The senior night staff nurse swallowed a yawn as she gave me our log, dangerous drug and medicine cupboard keys. 'Been one of those nights.'

'Won't take long to clear. Non-stop admissions?'

'No one in between three and five, which was a break as we were still clearing up the seven involved in a three-car pile-up around midnight. Four men to Albert, two girls to Catherine, one to I.C. [Intensive Care] and all still with us, *pro tem*. But the balloon really went up at ten past five. Twenty-two workmen.' She yawned hugely. 'The coach taking the early shift to some all-night building job tangled with a jack-knifing lorry loaded with steel girders.' She nodded at my expression. 'Yes. Messy.'

'Where've they gone?'

'Ten home after treatment. Six to Albert, three to Arthur, three to I.C. The last lad was only fit to shift a few minutes ago. We had to get all your men, apart from the S.A.O., out of their beds again. He was still up in his office doing the notes of the three-car job. He's still there working on the new lot, but the rest have gone back to their rooms. I was about to raise the poor man some tea. Can I leave that?'

'Sure. Sorry you've had it so rough. Sleep well.'

She smiled slightly. 'I won't sleep when I get to bed. I'll just bloody die of tiredness. Thanks.'

In the Receiving Room the girls had the floor and walls clean. After my explanation, Dolly demanded, 'If we've no patients, why extra staff?'

'God knows.' I pulled off my cuffs and unbuttoned my sleeves. 'As we don't know how long we've got, I'll do the work-list verbally. Nurses Jones and Henty, cubicles for immediate admissions, please—don't wait. Nurse Smithers, follow Nurse Jones. Nurse Fisher, show Nurse Donkin how to set the Shock Room. Nurses Fraser, Hedges and Black, re-stocking and testing all round, starting in here. I'll do laundry, desks, dispensary and outhouses.'

Donkin whispered to Fisher, 'How many immediate admissions are we expecting?'

'We aren't,' retorted Fisher, 'but we could have 'em any time. Watch the red bulbs over the doors. When they flash, we're in business.'

It was fifteen minutes before we had the room ready and I was free to check the outhouses—i.e. the offices, stock, linen, and other equipment rooms off our corridor. Sister's office was tidy. Peter's looked as though hit by a hurricane rather than a bomb as there were no blood stains. I put on a kettle while I straightened it up, made tea, knocked on Joss's closed door and went into his office without waiting for an answer.

'Good morning,' I said. 'Tea.'

He looked up from his writing with bloodshot eyes and the deliberation of old age. Even the condition of his uncharacteristically untidy hair had aged. It was dulled, lifeless. The front of his crumpled white coat was speckled with blood and there were ink stains on the right cuff. The mask round his throat was a limp paper frill. 'Thanks. I'm just finishing these notes. Then I hope to God the customers will let me get a bath, shave and some breakfast.' He fingered his blue chin very slowly. 'If not, I'll probably drop off over the next one in.'

'I can imagine.' I found a space for the tray and poured his tea. Seeing him like this had shaken me even more, if in another way, than Monday morning. He not only looked so much older and exhausted, he looked so vulnerable. 'I know you don't take sugar, but couldn't you use some?'

He smiled faintly, 'If you say so, Nursie—and don't mind my promptly throwing up on this carpet.'

I smiled and put down the tongs. 'Maybe you're right. You never did fancy sweeties.' I put the cup by his right hand. 'Sorry you had such a ghastly night, though I gather it's been pretty successful.'

He stiffened. 'We got 'em out of this Unit alive, but whether two of the chaps now in I.C. or their relatives'll thank us for saving them is an open question. One had two inches of driving mirror sticking out of his frontal lobe and the rest inside. The other poor bastard had his skull sliced open like a boiled egg. If I.C. do another great job on them,' he added bitterly, 'two nice human vegetables from here to eternity.'

I held on to the edge of the desk. 'Joss. I'm sorry. I didn't know.'

'Nor will the backroom boys if I don't finish these something notes for them. Shove me the log some time and I'll put 'em in.' The green light flashed. He reached the green receiver before me. 'Accident Unit, Desmond—oh? Yes, Sister, she's here.' He nodded to me to wait but did not hand over. 'Sorry, Sister, what was that? Oh!' His voice altered and his face clouded with anxiety. 'She is? I'm very sorry. Very.' He listened, frowning. 'Yes, I've thought so, too. Yes. Of course. We all will. Yes, right now.' He passed me the receiver. 'The Night Superintendent.'

'Bad news?' I mouthed, taking it.

'Bloody awful.' He picked up his pen and went back to his notes.

Miss Butler was warded in the Sisters' Home with query glandular fever. 'In Dr Gray's opinion,' said Night Super, 'no question of influenza, but this is only his provisional diagnosis.' She talked for quite a time. She did not mention leukaemia, but from what she said it was as omnipresent in Dr Gray's, Miss Evans', and her own mind as in mine. I watched Joss as I listened. Not only mine. I thought of Butler's colour, perpetual tiredness, thinness and snappy temper. All four did not have to be the forerunners of serious illness, but few were the serious illnesses without those early symptoms.

'Now, to deal with the Accident Unit, Nurse Maitland. I have just come from Miss Evans and have been asked to tell you she wishes you to take over temporarily as acting Sister Accidents. Do you feel you can manage?'

I felt paralytic with guilt and fear. 'Er—yes, Sister. That is, I hope so.'

'I'm sure you'll do nicely. Miss Mackenzie and the Office will, of course, give you every assistance. Mr Desmond has just promised every help from the residents—but our residents never let us down! Miss Evans will ring you when she is free to see you during the morning to discuss administrative details. All right?'

There was only one answer. 'Yes, thank you, Sister.'

'Thank you—Sister.'

I put down the receiver slowly. 'How old is she, Joss?'

He went on writing. 'Twenty-six.'

'I thought she looked much too tired. Has she always?'

'Not as much as recently.' He glanced up, briefly. 'So we're running the shop now?'

'Yes.' I was too shaken to be warned-off. 'Joss, I really am very sorry she's ill.'

He sighed, blotted the page, sat back and looked at me wearily. 'Stuff the placebos, Cathy, as I'm too bloody tired to swop 'em.'

'It wasn't a placebo, but if that's how you want to take it—'

'Christ, woman! I don't want to take anything or anyone—I just want to sleep for a week! As I can't, do me a favour—and don't say do I mean 'get lost' or I'll probably hit you.'

I believed him. 'What?'

'Do something about the atmosphere in this something Unit, or we'll all be queuing for beds in Florence and Stephen. I'm not a psychiatrist, so don't ask me why happy departments stay healthy. I just know they do. Get happiness-spreading. Get this dive an oasis of brotherly bloody

62

love, before some patient gets bumped off because the team's too short-handed and bloody-minded to do the job properly. And as this has to start at the top, you and I'll have to love each other. Get me?'

'Yes.'

'Good.' He took up his pen. 'With the news under your belt your happiness-spreading should be off to a head start.'

I turned at the door. 'I thought we had to love each other?'

He raised his triangular eyebrows. 'Passionately,' he said flatly, 'but even a decadent Englishman has his limits. Never before breakfast.'

I looked from his haggard face to his stained coat and the notes piled on his desk. 'That tea'll be stone cold if you don't drink it soon.' I went out and closed the door quietly.

Chapter Five

'I'm glad this repulsive weather is doing someone good.' Roxanne hitched her chair nearer the electric fire in our living room. 'When the camera crew and I got out of the 'plane yesterday and saw snow, we blamed the gin.'

Peter draped an arm along the sofa behind my shoulders and watched the hail hitting the window. 'One of the few patients we had in today swore blind his grandad had seen the Derby run in a snowstorm. Personally, I go along with Joss. Straight case of the Lord tempering the wind to the shorn lambs.'

'Lamb,' I said, 'singular.'

Roxanne glanced at me as she flicked back her long dark hair with both hands. We had talked most of last night, but Joss's name had only come up since Peter brought me home tonight. 'What's the latest on the sick Sister?'

Peter answered. 'Almost certainly glandular fever, though her blood count still isn't adding up as Charlie Gray'd like it. Time'll tell.'

I groaned. 'Leave the corn to the S.M.O., please!'

He flushed. 'You mean your middle name isn't Cassandra too, Cath?'

We had had a tremendous row over Butler. And as few

64

things can beat a guilt complex for putting people in bad tempers, initially, every member of the A.U. home staff had blamed everyone else for missing the diagnosis. This had consequently relaxed tension all round without any help from me, and given Joss an overwhelming psychological advance. In one of our note-writing sessions he said he didn't know whether he was more amused or sickened to find himself currently top of of the A.U. pops.

Miss Butler was now in Florence Small Ward. Joss visited her for a few minutes at least twice a day and made a particular point of telling us so. When we sent her flowers from the A.U., he had passed on her grateful thanks to the whole staff. The same evening doing the notes he told me that had he been Naomi, we'd have had our flowers back, stat, with a note telling us what we could do with them. 'Naomi was quite touched, but, of course, she had a temp. of 104 when they arrived.'

'Her temp.'s still swinging?'

'Yep. Was that chap Colin Arthur Morris driving the sports job or the estate car?'

'Sports. Thomas John Chester drove the estate.'

'Thanks.' He added the word then glanced across the desk I still thought of as 'Sister's.' 'Stan Lawson's doing all right. He hopes to be discharged in the next week, and have three weeks sick leave. He sent you his regards.'

'Good. Thanks for telling me.'

'As my old man and St Paul would say, faith, hope and charity—and the greatest of these is charity.' He smiled faintly. 'Strain killing you?'

'Not nearly so much,' I lied, 'as having Miss Mackenzie constantly on my neck.'

I thought over those note sessions whilst Peter explained to Roxanne why the cold snap had sent road accidents down and home accidents up. 'Long cold hours of daylight, so the weekend motorists stay home, get down to do-it-yourselves, fall off faulty step-ladders, dig chunks out of themselves with rusty chisels, or slice off their fingers with saws.'

'But you said you'd had a very slack weekend!'

'Compared to the normal holocaust of a normal July weekend, we have.' He saw her surreptitious check on the time. 'Sorry. Should've remembered nothing's so boring as other people's shop.'

'But I love hospital shop! I was only looking at the time as my agent said if she didn't ring by eleven tomorrow's job's on for sure. Do go on, please!' Roxanne turned to me. 'I wish he would, Cathy.'

'Go on, Pete. The girl needs a nice bedtime story seeing she's got to be up at four-thirty.'

'Four-thirty? You're not serious?'

Roxanne and I exchanged resigned glances. In the past we had both told Peter more times than we could remember that more often than not her job entailed getting up in the small hours as so many photographers preferred working by early morning light, or wanted a London setting when the streets were empty. I said, 'She's always creeping out between four and five. That's why she likes having early nights.'

'She doesn't like 'em,' corrected Roxanne, 'she just has to have 'em. If the camera doesn't lie, the swine accentuates. Unless I get enough sleep, the client'll take one look at the rushes and bellow "Get me another girl! I want my goods advertised, not the fact that some stupid cow needs pep pills!" Oh, hell!' Our telephone was ringing. It was in my bedroom, having been put there by a previous tenant. 'I'll bet that's my agent! I'll get it, Cathy.'

'I hope it isn't,' I said when she had gone. 'She's dead keen on tomorrow's job.'

Peter lit a cigarette. 'What's his name?'

'Why,' I said, 'why are men incapable of understanding that a girl can be dead keen on her job and just her job?'

'Hell—with her looks? There must be some man in her life.'

'Sure, rows, but none mean a thing to her—apart from her father. As he raised her alone after her mother died when she was ten, that's hardly surprising.'

'I'd forgotten him. Didn't you say he was an actor, or something?'

'Yes. He acted till his wife died, then started a drama school to stay put. Up north. He's doing very well. He was playing Cyrano when she was born—hence her name, and looks. I met him once. He's still staggeringly good-looking, tall as you but about half your width.' Roxanne was back, smiling. 'Still on?'

'Not my agent. For you. Mrs Desmond from darkest Kent. We had a nice chat about how glad we are you're back.'

'Mrs Desmond at this hour?' I shot into the bedroom convinced disaster had struck either my own or the Desmond family. Mrs Desmond only wanted me to spend my next free weekend at the vicarage. She had just been talking to Joss. 'He said this would be a good time to contact you. I wish he could come down too, but he says the residents are still only getting half-days. Such a worry for you all, this wretched 'flu. It's in every house in the village, but we've missed it so far—touch wood—oh dear —I know that's pagan but I must. And poor Naomi! But what a relief it is nothing worse than glandular fever. Such a nice child—very quiet—but very sweet. Joss brought her home several times last winter—I do enjoy it when the boys bring their girls down, though between ourselves, with Danny I do have difficulty keeping track of their names. I call them all "dearie"—so much safer. Can we expect you next weekend, Cathy? I do hope so as we'd love to see you and there is a little health matter I'd like your advice on. Not a word to Joss—' she added briskly, 'just between you and me.'

Knowing her age it was not hard to guess what that

was. I said I would love to get down for the day if I was not free all weekend, but it was possible I might be. One of the junior orthopaedic sisters was due to take over as Sister Accidents when she got back from holiday on Thursday. 'I've a couple of days off owing,' I added.

'So darling Joss said.'

Darling Joss had been a mine of information. She knew all about Stan Lawson's progress, Miss Kenton, the orthopaedic sister's name, and that Joss thought her a very nice and most efficient young woman—which was more than I knew.

'How nice,' I said.

'Isn't it, dear? I'm so pleased you two children are working together. Ruth will be amused! Must ring off now. See you soon!'

Roxanne went to bed a few minutes later. Peter left at midnight as that was one of the few rules on which our landlady had strong feelings. I was undressed and brushing my hair when Roxanne came in wearing her thickest winter housecoat and half a pound of cold cream on her face. 'The lad's changed a lot since I last saw him.'

I was surprised. 'I wouldn't have said so.'

'He has.' She was adamant. 'He's turned into a man. Want some tea?'

'Love some, but how about your rushes?'

'Not sleepy and I'm sick of staring at the ceiling. I can't take a sleeping pill this late or I'll look even worse.'

I swung round to face her. 'How long've you been taking sleeping pills?'

She had to think. 'I had a miserable bout of insomnia just after Christmas. A tame medic. I know gave me some. They've been a lot of help.'

'Sure. That's why you can't now sleep without 'em.'

'Cathy, I'm not hooked! I haven't asked him for another lot. I don't think they're particularly strong.' She went for the bottle. 'Are they?'

68

I shook out a couple. 'Yes. How many did he give you? Sixty, from the size of this bottle?' She nodded and I replaced the capsules. 'He warn you not to mix these with alcohol?'

'Yes. And that they'd make me a bit muzzy till they wore off. He said not to drive—things like that. He was very sensible—and so am I—so stop looking at me like that! I know what I'm doing!'

I lay back on my bed. 'Sure, you do! You're twenty-three. If you want to die at thirty, why shouldn't you?'

'One bottle of sleeping pills doesn't make me a junkie!'

'I didn't say it did. Yet. But if you now don't sleep so good unless you have these little knockouts, if I were you, I'd watch it. Did your tame medic. give you anything to counteract the muzziness?' Her expression answered me. 'Do I know him?'

'No. He's not from a London hospital.'

'Pity. I'd like him to drop in on our own friendly neighbourhood junkies at Martha's. Two jolly wards and a clinic open twenty-four hours a day that never lacks for customers. And every one of the poor kids originally started convinced they'd never get hooked—they could handle it. "Takes you into another world, see, Nurse. Releases like all the creative energies."' I paused, thinking back to my fourth year. 'Takes 'em into another world, all right. Only how do you create when you're dead?'

'Do stop talking about death!'

'You can't, if you're talking about drugs. Two go together. Like bacon-and-eggs.'

'Only if you're hooked on hard drugs.'

'Sure,' I said, 'but it's a proven fact that every addict, every single addict on the hard stuff, first started on the soft. And once you get on the hard drugs, lovey, you are going to die in about seven years. Maybe much less. Very occasionally, just a little longer.' I paused again, but she was silent. 'Those poor kids used to say "No worse than

69

tobacco or alcohol." Being an alcoholic doesn't do anyone any good, but it's a curable condition. Dying of carcinoma of the lung isn't much fun, but I've seen a good many die of it who've never smoked in their lives—though more who have. But I've never had to sit on the chest of a boy who's chucked smoking, to prevent his bashing his brains out against his headrail as he wants another cigarette.' I locked my hands behind my head. 'Some of the girls were my age. Lots from good homes—on paper. They didn't look like girls. Dirty old women until we cleaned them up. Then just emaciated old women.'

Her brown eyes stood out blackly against the white cream. She jiggled the capsules in their bottle. 'Honestly, knockouts?' I nodded. 'I'd better show you my pep pills. I've only taken about three of them. They make me feel odd.'

When I saw them, that did not surprise me. 'Did your tame medic. qualify in the U.K.?'

'Yes. He's English.' She hesitated. 'Shove both lots down the bog?'

'And your tame medic. with them.'

We had first met when she had her appendix out in Catherine during my second year. A year later we met again by chance at a party. Roxanne had just found our present flat, and I wanted to live out but couldn't get digs I could afford near enough to Martha's. Our flat was a fifteen-minute walk away.

We gave it three months on trial as we barely knew each other and our jobs were so different. We found we got along very well, possibly as we both insisted on going our separate ways, but also as our jobs turned out to have a surprising amount in common. Odd and often long hours; irregular days off; no automatic right to free weekends; and in both unpunctuality on the job was a major crime. In consequence, it suited us equally to keep the flat reasonably tidy and unavoidable chores up to date.

70

We never borrowed each other's clothes or men, if only, as we agreed, because Roxanne was six inches taller than me and we liked totally opposite types. When one of us was entertaining the other kept out of the living-room unless the guest was someone like Peter and part of the establishment. But if either had an unwelcome guest, we did one of the best sister acts in the business. That only once failed; I had rung Peter and he had rushed round as chucker-out. It had made his week, as the limpet had been an ex-steady of Roxanne's who had once been very rude to him.

The temperature shot up that night. Next day summer was back to normal and so was our Monday admission rate. By early afternoon the four new medic. students were wilting visibly. They asked Mr Palmer if it was always like this?

'No, no, dear boys!' He pulled down his mask to mop his face. 'They're only coming in one at a time, today. We only call ourselves busy when they come in by the half-dozen. Not today.'

'Mr Palmer,' I said, 'please, please, don't tempt providence!'

'Not providence, Sister—' he leered amiably as he scrubbed at the sink besides me—'but how about you?'

Joss was washing at my other side. 'Not a chance, Dave. "Unmoved, cold, and to temptation slow." Goes with the job. Right, Sister?'

'Handed out with the Sister's belt, Mr Desmond. You going to get some lunch now we've actually stopped?'

'Seems like a good idea—oh Gawd!' The red light flashing. 'Open your big mouth like that again, Dave, and I'll take you apart with the nearest scalpel and chuck the pieces to Miss Mackenzie for closer grinding.' He dried his hands and read over my shoulder the memo sheet handed me by Nurse Smithers. 'This poor old girl's been lying on the floor since Saturday night, Nurse?'

'That's what the ambulance men told Mr Jarvis, Mr Desmond. In a very neglected condition, they said. The police broke in after the postman saw her lying in the hall when he was pushing a thick circular through her letter-box. She lives alone and the neighbours hadn't noticed she hadn't got her milk in.'

I caught Dolly's eye. 'In C2, please.' I glanced at Joss. 'Sorry about your lunch.'

'Doesn't matter. Lost my appetite.'

The old lady was a Mrs Jennings. She was seventy-nine, very overweight, with arthritis in both legs. She had caught 'flu last week and as she had not called any doctor, it had turned to pneumonia. Her fall down the stairs had fractured her left femur. She had sewn herself into three sets of underclothes and was so infested that even her eyebrows were affected.

Miss Mackenzie paid one of her now habitual visits to the room as Dolly and Nurse Fisher in special gowns were sealing Mrs Jennings' clothing in the large, sturdy brown paper bags provided for this purpose. Mrs Jennings had been moved to a side ward in Intensive Care, Joss had gone to his belated lunch, and I was carbolizing C2's table.

'Don't let me disturb you, Sister.' Miss Mackenzie stood at the foot of the table. She looked at the row of buttons and the rest of the high-powered equipment. 'We pride ourselves on our progress, but Lord Lister would feel at home, just now, in more ways than one. I doubt he was confronted by a more distressingly neglected patient when he first used the carbolic spray in Glasgow Royal Infirmary over one hundred years ago. 1867 as I recall. 1971. Men can be placed on the moon, but in this great city old folk can be found in this condition. Progress? H'mmm.' She waited till I had finished then came with me whilst I changed gowns and washed my hands. I was growing so accustomed to her at my elbow that I only dropped the soap once. 'I was sorry to send a patient in that condition to this department,' she said very quietly, 'but as Dr Gray was forced to admit, officially we should not have accepted her. She should have been transferred to a geriatric hospital. Did Mr Desmond object?'

'Only on her account, Sister.' I did not repeat his private comments to me as they were unrepeatable. 'Directly he examined her he insisted she go straight to Intensive Care.'

'You warned Sister Intensive Care?'

'That she was dirty? Yes, Sister.'

'Good.' Her stern face relaxed slightly. 'It is most fortunate that our Senior Accident Officer is officially permitted to share the Senior Medical and Surgical Officers' privilege of admitting patients on his own authority, but unlike the two senior residents has no overall responsibility for the total bedstate. I have observed Mr Desmond to be a humane as well as sound surgeon. I assured Dr Gray Mrs Jennings would be admitted without question. I'm much relieved.'

I was torn between fascination and disgust by this insight into the works of bureaucracy. 'Sister, otherwise, we couldn't have taken her in?'

'St Martha's has only one geriatric ward and that is full, Sister.'

'I see.' I didn't, but I had to say it. 'In Mr Desmond's opinion she should do quite well. Sister, what'll happen when she goes out as she seems to have no living relatives?'

'I have already contacted our senior social worker. That will be attended to, Sister. Very well.' She nodded to herself. 'Thank you.'

Later, I handed this on to Joss. 'Did you guess we were being used as a side door?'

'Yep.'

'You didn't say!'

'Not my job to teach you yours. Anyway, she had to come in.' He scratched his neck. 'I ate most of my lunch under a shower, but I'm still itching.'

'I feel I'm crawling.'

His eyes danced for the first time since that Saturday night. 'Togetherness, at last!'

I could have kicked myself had my knees not suddenly felt so weak. 'Can Mr Geddes take over the plaster room? Mr Kovac should've been off an hour ago. He'll never go if I don't push him out and he is looking awfully tired.'

'I'll tell Geddes. You don't think Kovac's getting the bug?'

'His temp. was normal when I took it this morning. I think it's just middle age.'

'I hope you're right. I like our elegant Pole and the only man I've seen slap on a better plaster is Hoadley East.'

I handed that one on. 'Don't let on that I have, Mr Kovac.'

The plaster technician's lined leathery face creased into one of his rare smiles. 'I enjoy my work, Sister, but appreciation is always pleasant.' He managed to bow elegantly in a flapping gown, long white plastic apron and white tennis shoes. 'It will remain our secret—but I am in no hurry to go. I finish that young man's plaster.'

'Mr Geddes is just coming and he'll do it. You must go off, Mr Kovac, or you'll be ill. And what will the A.U. do without you?'

Mr Geddes was small, fair, willing, but nervous. So he bustled in, importantly. 'Right! What's to do?'

Joss had arrived. 'Wheel in that chap on the right, lad.' He took off his white coat. 'Mind if I keep my hand in, Mr Kovac? Once, long long ago, it was rumoured that I crossed the river to be an orthopaedic registrar.'

'Sister, sorry—' Nurse Fisher cantered in. 'Mrs Hicks is in a tiz. She's suddenly discovered she must've left her

74

handbag in the ambulance as she remembers them picking it up when they put her on the stretcher, but not bringing it in here. It hasn't much money in it, but her brother's telephone number at work is in her diary. She's just remembered he asked her to collect his kids from school and they'll be out in a few minutes.'

Mrs Hicks had mild concussion and shock after being knocked down by a girl parking a scooter and was behind drawn curtains in Bed 4 in the Shock Room. The scooter-driver was resting in 5 after having her right clavicle replaced. Both women were later going home in hospital cars.

The handbag had slipped down between Mrs Hicks' mattress and headrail. I rang the head teacher first. He said I could rest assured he would attend to the matter forthwith, and with every respect, Sister, if anything frightened him more than a woman behind a steering-wheel, it was a woman on a mechanically operated two-wheeler. Mrs Hicks' brother was glad his sister was not badly hurt, but he couldn't say he was surprised as she never would wear her glasses. 'That's you ladies, all over! All you think of is looking pretty for us mere males and God bless you for it, say I, for one!'

I wondered momentarily with whom Women's Lib would have the tougher struggle and decided on Mrs Hicks' brother as it takes imagination and maturity to feel and admit fear.

The rush hour had begun when the Receiving Room red light next flashed. Joss, Peter and Mr Geddes came in together almost immediately, and bringing with them the faint and rather sickly smell of wet plaster. They had listened-in on the Smithers-Jarvis conversation on the plaster room red 'phone. Messrs Charlesworth and Palmer who arrived a minute later had caught it in the rest room.

'Seven, eh?' Mr Charlesworth gloomily studied the huge off-duty rota pinned to the green baize board against the wall above the standing desk. 'Why do the morons have to try and overtake in the rush hour? There goes my early evening. Yours too, Sister?'

'Looks that way, Mr Charlesworth.'

I was down as off at six, but Dolly and I had already arranged that I would stay on till she got back at seven. It was Henty's day off, and though Roberts was a good senior student, she wasn't even an acting staff nurse and it was Monday. Smithers was still too new and the other girls too junior to help Roberts run the department alone. I paired Roberts with Mr Charlesworth, asked Smithers to stay on 'lights and messages' and felt a new sympathy for Butler as I saw the look the girls exchanged.

Joss was watching me. Just after, waiting for the ambulances, he asked, 'Roses or carnations?'

'Roses, please.'

By half past eight all seven men had been moved to the wards. I left Dolly to do the notes with Joss when he got back from supper. On my way out I met Dr Gray in Emergencies' hall. As always now, he enquired mournfully after my own and the A.U. staff's health and advised me to see we all kept up the extra vitamin tablets and took at least a ten-minute brisk walk in the fresh air every day. 'Don't forget, Sister, sensible prevention can well prevent the necessity for cure!'

'I won't forget, Doctor. And how are you?'

He was a dapper little man with the face of a highly intelligent and kindly rat. 'I think I'm well, thank you, Sister. Can't say I've had time to reflect on the matter. Do I look well?'

I smiled. 'Yes, Doctor.'

'Good, good,' he said sadly. 'I haven't a spare male medical bed tonight.'

Chapter Six

I was late off, but Miss Mackenzie was later. 'In and out till we closed,' said Dolly.

'Like this morning.'

'And when you were off this afternoon. She hung till we suddenly emptied ten minutes ago. We can't be doing things wrong or she'd have said so. Maybe she's just decided she likes the A.U. better than Emergencies?'

I shook my head, thoughtfully. This was beginning seriously to worry me. It had made sense in my first week, but being well into my second with only one more full day in charge, I would have expected—and hoped—Miss Mackenzie's visits would have decreased. The reverse had happened. 'She doesn't like accident work. She told me the other night she's too old for it now. She said it took the stamina of youth as well as training to withstand the pressure. She thinks that's why we haven't an Accident Consultant on the Staff. All our present pundits qualified before this place was opened and though she didn't say it, I gathered they wouldn't touch the job if you gave it to them with a plastic rose. If Michael Roth makes the Staff maybe he'd take it on, having been an S.A.O., but having been one—why ask for his coronary in the late thirties instead of the usual late forties?'

'Mother Mack tell you all that?' I nodded. She propped her elbow on my desk, her chin on her hand and flapped her eyelashes. 'Ooh duckie! She fancies you!'

I smiled. 'Oh no! If she has a weakness—which could be denied—it's for a braw laddie in a white coat. She once told Hill [Butler's predecessor] that at the risk of seeming prejudiced she was forced to admit there was no nicer laddie than a nice young Scots doctor.'

'I know why she's haunting us! She fancies Mr Geddes! Our Hamish! Wait till I tell him!'

'Don't you dare! The poor boy's terrified enough of her as it is! He was so ham-strung by her watching him cut off a leg plaster this morning, the ends of his tie somehow got caught in the shears and he had to cut half of it off to save himself from strangulation.'

She slapped a hand over her mouth to stifle her shout of laughter. 'What did Mother Mack say?'

I mopped my eyes. 'She didn't. She just looked at him.'

Peter ambled through the open doorway. 'What's happened to the customers? And why the unseemly levity?'

I caught Dolly's eye. 'Just having a jolly handing over report.'

Joss was back from tea. 'What've you done with them all?' He peered round my office as if expecting to see patients stacked on the filing cabinets. 'Tuesday and the rush hour's started. Damned unhealthy.'

I jerked my head at the sudden red flashing above the door and listened-in on the red receiver. Dolly whispered, 'Health restored, Mr D.,' and he gave her a thumbs down sign.

The evening was busy and Miss Mackenzie was with us for most of it. Next morning was busier. She did not come in once. By lunch time, Mr Geddes and I were equally unnerved.

Dolly and George Charlesworth were back on dating

terms. Later, Dolly vowed she had told him to keep it quiet and he'd only let it out to Dave Palmer who swore he'd just mentioned it to only one of the medic. students. In the event, before the first patient came in that morning, the entire A.U. staff knew for a fact Hamish Geddes was the dead spit of the great and long-gone love of Miss Mackenzie's life, a gallant little Highland M.O. last seen playing his bagpipes when not operating single-handed on the beaches at Dunkirk. Poor little Mr Geddes went puce behind his mask every time the double doors swung open. He only relaxed after lunch when Joss sent him to work in the plaster room. His relief was short-lived as we promptly had an in-rush and had to get him back.

A girl who had broken her left arm falling down some narrow, stone basement steps and a hefty young Irishman in semi-coma and with a badly slashed face came in together. The Irishman had been carried to the hospital by five of his mates. They sat red-faced, anxious and exuding beer fumes in our relatives' rest-room. They said the patient was a Michael Joseph Murphy, aged thirty-one, and wouldn't hurt a baby unless he'd the drink taken. 'One jar and there's no holding him back at all.'

Mr Palmer asked how many jars Murphy had had before the fight started?

The mates were appalled. 'Mother of God, Doctor, would a decent man be counting?'

Mr Geddes and Nurse Smithers were with the girl in C3, Mr Charlesworth and Nurse Henty with a West Indian railwayman in C4. He had a hairline skull fracture and some very bad bruises, but had been incredibly lucky. A car with faulty brakes had run straight into him as he was correctly crossing a light-controlled pedestrian crossing. He had been flung right over the car and landed head down on the opposite pavement. He was twenty-one and a keen amateur boxer. He probably owed his luck equally to both.

Murphy was in C5, as C1 and C2 were awaiting seriously injured men on their way in. After his initial examination, Joss beckoned Mr Palmer. 'Dead drunk and no other damage I can find, but get a picture of his head and let me see it. Fix that face. All yours, Dave.'

Mr Palmer crossed himself. 'Sir, ever so dear sir, can I have danger money, please?'

'Leave it to me. I'll see your next-of-kin gets it. Get a medic. to help you.'

I said, 'And Nurse Fisher, Mr Desmond? Nurse Hedges can run the Shock Room.'

Joss hesitated then smiled. 'Yep. Good idea.'

Fisher was my size, red-haired and the prettiest girl in the A.U. Mr Palmer said he was lost, but lost. 'It's not that I'm anti-feminist, Sister—nay, I'm all for the burning of bras—they do so get in the way—but I just think a pretty little dolly doesn't look her best without her teeth.'

Joss said, 'If Murphy surfaces to find a pretty little dolly holding his hand, chances are no one'll lose their teeth. Use force on a surfacing drunk his size and his won't be the only face that needs about fifteen stitches. Also there's over a thousand quid's worth of equipment in this cubicle.'

I went for Fisher. Joss came out of 4 as she disappeared round the drawn side curtain of 5. The only innovation I had made was to return to the former Sister Accident's custom of always keeping the end curtains of occupied cubicles open as I shared her view that this made super-vision and movement easier. Etiquette insisted I ask Joss if he objected. He hadn't. 'We closed them at Benedict's, but when in Rome . . .' was all he said. He had shown the same adaptability from the morning I took over. He never now referred to the A.U. as 'the Unit', used any but Martha's jargon, or wore his Benedict's tie. This made my job a lot easier, even if it underlined with a new clarity his earlier belligerence on Butler's behalf. I hadn't much time to let this bother me, but I remained aware that I had shoved it to to the back of some mental cupboard, just as I did with clothes to which I had suddenly taken a dislike. I could then forget the things existed. I hoped it would work as well with Joss, but as I didn't dislike him realized I was giving hope a tough job.

The expected patients again arrived simultaneously in separate ambulances. One, a bricklayer's mate, had fallen thirty feet onto rough ground, and had a fractured pelvis and some ugly lacerations, but his head was unhurt. The second man had been driving a heavy lorry that had hit the side of a road bridge and then overturned. He had multiple injuries and his condition was dangerous. He went into C1.

Joss had about two minutes in which to tell Mr Charlesworth what he wanted done for the bricklayer's mate. I caught Nurse Black's eye, mouthed 'Medic.' and nodded at C5 then C2. She nodded back and swiftly collected Mr Palmer's assistant and joined Henty and the J.A.O. in C2.

Eight of us worked together on the man in C1: Joss, Peter, a pathologist, radiographer, Mr Geddes, Smithers, two medic. students, and myself. The only person who spoke at all, and only very occasionally, was Joss. He and I were working on the man's ripped open abdomen. Peter had him anaesthetized. The pathologist and one student were setting up a blood transfusion in his left ankle. The second student was cutting off the left, and apparently less damaged, side of his clothes. Smithers was very carefully cutting the right trouser leg as shafts of bone were glinting through the sodden thick material. Mr Geddes was cleaning surgically the right leg. The radiographer, a girl, was swinging the heavy portable around for the necessary X-rays as if working a box camera.

Someone lightly touched my shoulder. 'Just to say, please ignore us, Sister. Forgive the interruption, Mr

Desmond.' Miss Evans, our Chief Nursing Officer, stepped back to Miss Mackenzie waiting about a yard from the table. Neither spoke to us again and I had no idea how long they stood there. Afterwards Fisher said for about ten minutes. Joss did not recall seeing them at all.

I had thought Fisher good, but I had not realised how good until that afternoon. Nurse Donkin, the new third year, was 'lights and messages'. Fisher was the same set, but while Henty and I were tied up, Fisher took over as well as a good senior staff nurse. The porters arrived and removed the West Indian and the girl in C3 to wards. Murphy surfaced and began muttering angrily.

'There, there,' said Fisher's voice, 'there, there. You're all right, dear. No, don't try and sit up. You had a little accident, you're in a hospital, I'm a nurse—the doctor's just stitching a little cut on your face—quietly now—just hold onto my hand. . . .'

Mr Charlesworth appeared beside Joss. 'I'd say mine's ready to shift to I.C. Shall I carry on here whilst you look?'

'Yes.' Both men stripped off their gloves and put on clean. When Joss returned from C2 they did so again. After a heavy day our used-gloves count often ran into three figures. 'Go with him, George,' said Joss.

Donkin was hovering. I nodded twice. She vanished to ring the lodge for porters and the special I.C. trolley and the ward to say a patient was on the way. Shortly after she was back with a memo sheet. She held it out for me to read without altering my position.

I said, 'Mr Desmond, female, seventy-one, fractured right tib. and fib. on the way in. Home accident.'

'Palmer. I want the J.A.O. here.' And when Mr Charlesworth returned. 'He can use another drip. High in that left arm, George.'

A little later the drips and blood were running in well and the internal haemorrhage had stopped. Joss asked,

'Sister, do we know anything about this chap beyond the name on his driving licence?'

'His home's in Manchester. The police have contacted his wife and she's coming down as soon as some relative arrives to look after their three children.'

'Hold it!' Peter spoke sharply. 'Foot's going up to top.'

We all froze as if playing grandmother's footsteps, and watched Peter. 'Stopped.' He pulled off his stethoscope with one hand, pulled forward the scarlet-framed 'crash' trolley with the other. Joss had come to life, had his gloves off and started cardiac massage.

Giving cardiac massage is very exhausting. Whilst the qualified men took it in turns, Henty and I kept the man's injuries at blood-heat and Smithers kept the sterile saline we were using at the right temperature. That entailed constant topping up and changing of the bowls in the double-bowl stands. Once, a medic. student asked, 'Will you have to open up his chest wall?'

'If necessary,' Joss grunted, 'but it shouldn't be as he's started again. He should be able to manage on his own soon.'

He was right. 'Good.' He stood back, pulled off his sodden mask, dried his face with it, and chucked it away breathing as if he had run a mile in two minutes. 'How's he your end, Peter?'

'Nicely.'

Another pint of blood had run in before Joss murmured, 'Do we know their ages, Sister?'

'All under five. Two boys, one girl.'

He didn't say more. We worked on in silence till the man was fit to move to I.C. Peter, George Charlesworth and Henty went with him. The rest of us removed gloves, masks and stained gowns in that same silence. It held an element that was hard to define and was present in all the faces when the masks came off. It was one I had noticed before, on both sides of the Atlantic, after what went down in the notes as 'successful therapy for cardiac arrest'. It wasn't triumph, satisfaction, or even relief, as most of us knew death too well to underestimate the strength of the opposition. It was not unconnected with the fact that the name Lazarus made instant sense to anyone with the sketchiest Christian upbringing, and particularly so now. Lazarus had been a young man when he was raised from the dead.

Miss Evans sent for me that night. The day report from Intensive Care was uppermost on her desk when the Office Sister ushered me in and ominously closed the door on her way out. I had been too tired to be over-shaken by Miss Evans' summons, but when she asked me to sit down, the combination shattered me. In Martha's it could only mean one of two things: bad personal news, or a professional bouquet.

Miss Evans was smiling. 'I gather you had a little trouble with that man in Cubicle 1 after Miss Mackenzie and I left you this afternoon. But Sister Intensive Care says he seems to have settled down quite nicely tonight.'

I breathed more naturally. 'I'm so glad.'

'Of course.' She went on to ask me to stay in Butler's job until she was fit to return. 'Possibly two or three months, possibly more. Glandular fever can take a long time to clear up. No objections? Good. I admit I can ill spare Miss Kenton from the Orthopaedic Block and, on reflection, see no occasion to alter present arrangements in the Accident Unit. But one point must be made clear, Sister!' She then lectured me sternly on the subject of off-duty, said I must have this Saturday off and Miss Kenton would relieve me for the day and next week, when Staff Nurse White returned, from midday Friday to midday Monday. 'All right, Sister? Good girl.' As I stood up, she added with the lack of formality that was one of the many reasons for her popularity, 'Now I'll tell you something that'll make you forget your poor feet,

84

Sister. You may share it with your staff. It is Miss Mackenzie's considered opinion that our present Accident Unit is a credit to St Martha's. Thank you, my dear. Goodnight.'

1 tottered back to my office and since we were finally empty, into my chair. A mountain of notes was waiting. I just stared at them. Joss was at supper. I wondered how he would like being a credit to St Martha's and smiled, foolishly.

Peter put his head round the door. 'What did she want?'

We were still oozing smugness when Joss returned and infuriated me by saying he had known I was staying on for the last two days. 'How can you be so mean? Why didn't you tell me?'

'Union rules, dearie.' He began sorting notes. 'Why don't you go home? Nurse Henty can manage these.'

I hesitated. 'Take hours.'

'She's a bright girl. Good experience for her.'

Peter said Joss was right and he'd get a porter to get me a taxi as he was on-call. 'All you look fit for now is bed, Cath. Just wish I could take you there myself.'

'There, there, dear boy, ever so there, there.' Joss had Dave Palmer's voice perfectly. 'Keep it cool. Get going, woman!' He looked up at Peter then back at me. 'Don't worry. If necessary, I'll get Nurse Fisher to hold his hand.'

Chapter Seven

'There's no need for you to stay as long as myself, dear.'
Mrs Desmond adjusted the angle of her ginger straw in
the hall mirror. It was less than a yard wide. 'The Vicar
has to see Tom Mercer about the guttering on the Lady
Chapel roof and will run you back. I must stay till the end
or umbrage will be taken as they stay for ours.' She
glanced at the closed study door, then added quietly,
'I'm sure the old ticker's fine and it's just indigestion, but
as your father always said—when in doubt, see an expert.
You're certain this won't get you into any trouble?'

'Positive! I'll have to do it through Miss Evans, but
both she and Dr Lincoln Browne will understand you
want to be reassured without worrying your family.'

She put a hand on my shoulder. 'Darling, am I fussing
about nothing? Is it just my age and because my children
have grown up and gone?'

I suddenly felt very old. 'I think you're being very
sensible. If you were Mum, I'd have said exactly what I
did this morning.' The study door was opening. 'Feeling
strong, Vicar?'

We were going to the annual summer church fête in
the next parish. Mr Desmond's aversion to fêtes was an
old family joke and on his own admission the reason why

his own was always successful. He left it entirely to his P.C.C. and his wife.

'Strengthened by a sense of duty and sublime sensation of self-righteousness, Cathy. Ready, my dear?'

The road ran through fields of young green hops climbing forests of poles, and corn now golden but in places still flattened by last week's hail and heavy rain. The sun was warm without being hot and all the elders were in flower. The parish lay away from the marsh and the last stretch of road had originally been laid by the Romans along the crest of a wooded hill. The wood was still there, too. The overhanging branches cut out the sun and the light was cool and green as in the depths of the sea.

The fête was in the vicarage garden and two Special Constables were directing the traffic coming and going from the car park in the field opposite. One was Bert Mercer. 'Back again are you, then?'

'Bert, why are you supporting the rival firm? Peace been declared?'

He smiled slowly and mopped his broad face with a glaringly white handkerchief. Mrs Bert once worked in a laundry. 'You'd not reckon that if you was along the Lamb, tonight. Still, they said did I mind? Well, it seemed right.'

The two villages had fought each other on Saturday nights and Bank Holidays for as long as anyone could remember. No one knew why. It had never prevented inter-marriages. The same surnames were listed on the war memorials in both churchyards.

'The same names,' mused Mr Desmond, 'would've been listed after Agincourt and Crecy, had any man bothered to make such a list. And when not fighting the French, they'd still have belted the daylights out of each other.' He surveyed the back lawn crowded with the inhabitants of both villages. 'The English have a deep affection for their old tribal customs. But one aspect invariably puzzles me on these occasions. From whence do all these worthy ladies wearing coloured meringues on their heads come and to where do they disappear, between fêtes? I never see them in church.'

'Oh, yes, Vicar! Think of Harvest Festival. They all come. There's barely standing room.'

He smiled over his glasses. '*Mea culpa.* I have overlooked that most cherished old tribal—or to be accurate pagan—custom.'

The cake stall was under a chestnut bowed with white candles; the fancy goods, under an ash; the pick-the-right-card-and-win-a-bottle stall discreetly arranged by the hedge at the bottom of the garden. The hard-working tea ladies coping with the insatiable demand for nourishment from within two minutes of the official opening raced round their tent growing redder as their urns grew emptier and the butter in the bridge rolls turned to oil.

Mr Desmond savoured his. 'Butter. From George Mercer's herd.'

One of about fifteen Mercers sitting near overheard. He was a tall fair teenager who could have been Bert's son, had Bert had sons and not only daughters. 'That's right, Vicar. Me Dad sent it up. How'd you reckon?'

Mr Desmond nodded at a distant farmhouse just visible through the trees. 'What's that farm there called, lad?'

The boy looked superior and his elder relatives amused. 'Martin's, 'course. Didn't you know that, then?'

'Yes, and I should, seeing I was born there. Old Mr Martin, whom your grandad'll remember, was my grandad. Your grandad was the best young stockman he ever had, and he taught me the taste of a good butter. Brigadier Bell bought the farm twenty years ago from the man who bought it after my grandad died.'

The clan chuckled appreciatively. 'Walked into that one didn't you, young Trev? He knows, does the Vicar.' They eyed the host vicar, an incomer, much as the A.U. staff had Naomi Butler. 'Makes a difference.'

The shooting gallery, an innovation to me, was tucked round the side of the front garden and doing the best business of the day. Brigadier Bell was loading the guns, his wife organizing the queues of men, boys and a few girls, with crisp firmness. The size of her pink linen hat was rivalled only by Mrs Desmond's. They were old patients and friends of my parents. We exchanged glad cries as they were too busy for more.

'The Established Church,' observed Mr Desmond as we strolled on, 'has always been gifted with a very practical sense of priorities.'

We had agreed to leave before the official entertainment began, but the middle of the lawn had been cleared and the little children started country dancing while he was still shaking the necessary hands. For years, the three Desmonds, my brother and I had danced on the Desmonds' lawn. The parental bribery rate had risen as we approached nine, the maximum age. At eight, Ruth and I had collected two choc-ices from my father, two lollies from the vicar, half a pound of jelly babies from my mother, and a pound of apples to salvage our teeth from Mrs Desmond.

In the car, I said, 'We'd eaten the lot before you'd announced who got the most points bowling for the turkey. We weren't sick, but I can't think why not.'

He smiled. 'Your father used to say about the only thing a healthy child's stomach can't digest is cast-iron.' He paused, shortly. 'I still miss him, sadly, Cathy, as of course you do. He was a good man who did much good with his life. And he was my friend. God willing, we shall meet again.' He glanced sideways and answered my thoughts. 'Yes. I do, though perhaps not at your age. Youth has so much faith in itself, that it often seems to feel the need of no other. Once youth's brief glory has burnt out, if one has the blessed good fortune to be given the gift of Faith, one does not underestimate its necessity.

Ah—Tom's van waiting!' He slowed to a stop and gave
me his front door key. 'Leave it on the latch. You'll be all
right on your own?'

'Fine, thank you. And for the outing.'

His older, thinner, more aesthetic face, smiled Joss's
smile. 'Thanks to your pleasant companionship I enjoyed
it much more than I anticipated, and many would add,
deserved. With you shortly!'

I looked at our old house as I let myself in. It did not
hurt as much as I expected, but the empty vicarage hurt
much more. I could see Joss standing in the study on that
other Saturday night and myself drifting round all the
next day, like some naïve teenager in a fantasy world
where Love was Real and nothing to do with sex. Sex was
something the biology mistress shoved down one's throat
in those constant 'straight from the shoulder' chats that
embarrassed her as much as it bored the class. I
remembered Ruth and myself moaning, 'Sex, again! Oh,
God—that drag!'

I found a rug and cushions and went out into the
garden. Just beyond the pond, between the willows and
the apple trees, there was a patch of rough grass that
under one of the unwritten laws children observe amongst
themselves had been 'the girls' patch'. It was invisible
from both houses and had the new advantage of being
free of associations with Joss.

I kicked off my shoes, watched the sky filtering through
the apple leaves and thought about the fête. That was a
mistake, as Mr Desmond's behaviour reminded me of
Joss's at Ruth's reception. I switched to the A.U. and
wondered how Miss Kenton was getting on. She had
come in yesterday for a few hours to get into the routine.
She was a tall, rather striking girl in her mid-twenties
with very dark hair and the slightly hearty, slightly insensitive air of a good head girl. 'Right,' she'd said, 'what's to
do? You name it, m'dear. You're boss!'

The 'flu epidemic was beginning to subside, but the senior registrars were still down to one day and one night off, instead of their alternate free weekends. On paper this was Joss's. Mr Roth's deputy, Mr Carr, was standing in for him tomorrow. One of the registrar anaesthetists was taking over for Peter today. Peter had wanted me to go home with him to soothe his mother as she thought it was time he married. When he didn't bring a girl home, she always produced some daughter of one of her friends.

A moorhen rustled across the pond. A blackbird in the nearest apple tree was singing like a nightingale. One summer evening in my first year I had got home for the evening before my days off to find Joss with my father in the garden. Joss had looked in to say goodbye before going back to Benedict's after a holiday. A patient had arrived, Joss and I had stayed in the garden and counted seven nightingales singing in chorus.

I had had a surfeit. I closed my eyes to shut out thought and was asleep almost immediately. I woke when someone gently touched my face. I smiled, stretched out my arms and blinked, expecting to see Mrs Desmond. Joss's face was a few inches from mine.

For about five seconds I wasn't sure if I was awake or asleep. We stared at each other with an equal kind of incredulity. I had to touch him to be certain and put my hands on his shoulder. 'It's you?'

He kissed me so wonderfully that at first I was incapable of coherent thought. Then I got my face free. 'If you're that hungry, go and make yourself a meal!'

He raised himself a little and his colour altered. 'If you don't want it, don't set it up!'

'I did *not*! I thought you were your mother!' I pushed him off without difficulty as he was standing up. 'You should be in the A.U.! Why aren't you?'

He had propped himself against an apple tree and was now equally angry, though he controlled it better.

'Worked out easier for John Carr to take over this afternoon and tomorrow morning.'

'How was I supposed to know that?' I slung the rug over my shoulder and glared at him. 'Your parents didn't say you were coming.'

'They didn't know till I turned up. Didn't know myself till lunch. The parents don't expect a warning. This happens to be their—and my—home.'

'Where I thought vicar's lad's Union Rules obtained. Oh, sure, I know—what are old pals for but to help out? Tell you what, Joss—I'll buy you your very own teddy bear.'

He flushed. 'You've made your point, duckie.'

'So I should hope!' I was shaking with rage. 'Providing you with a therapeutic release doesn't give me one single frisson!'

He looked me over. 'Snap, darling.'

'Children, there you are!' Mrs Desmond joined us, beaming. 'Isn't this a lovely surprise, Cathy? Such a pity Joss has to go back tonight, but as he's promised, of course, he must and he can give you a lift—'

'I've got a cheap day return—'

'A bit of a waste, darling, but so much nicer to drive back on this lovely evening. Such a long drive alone. He'll love to take you. Won't you, Joss?'

He looked at me. 'Always happy to help out an old pal.'

'That's settled! Come along. Supper's ready!'

'Supper?' I looked at my watch. It was seven. 'I've slept hours! I'm so sorry, Mrs Desmond—'

'Now, why? You needed the rest. Joss and his father had a nice quiet tea, then Joss fetched me. Gervase said you were still sleeping when we got back, but we had to wake you now as Joss has to be back by ten.'

I asked, 'Not on call tonight, Joss?'

'No, but I've got a heavy date.'

At supper, after the P.M. on the fête, the subject was

Naomi Butler. Mr Desmond was glad to hear that nice young woman was progressing well. 'How much longer should she be warded, Joss?'

'Week or so. Then a very long sick leave.'

'Malta?' Mrs Desmond turned to me. 'Did you know Naomi's parents have retired out there? Such a beautiful island, I believe. Joss was out there for his last summer's holiday.'

'How nice,' I said.

'It was,' said Joss. 'Naomi and I did our best to miss the return flight. Mum, I hate to rush off, but as we've got over fifty miles . . .'

Mrs Desmond saw us off as someone had called to see her husband. 'Don't forget, Joss, if Naomi would like a quiet week with us before she flies off, we'll love to have her.'

'Thanks, Mum, I'll tell her.' He kissed her and got into his car.

Mrs Desmond kissed me. 'You'll let me know?' she whispered.

'Soon as it's fixed,' I answered as quietly. 'Don't worry too much. He's a very nice and quite brilliant man. I'd take my heart across the world to him. You'll like him.'

She kissed me again. 'Come back soon.'

Joss had the engine on and was fiddling with his safety-belt. He could not have overheard us, but he watched his mother very thoughfully in the driving mirror as he drove off. 'She's looking much too tired. You notice?'

'Yes. Missing Ruth.'

'Typical! Typical trained nurse's reaction! Fatigue must have a psychosomatic origin! No question of the cause being organic, or very possibly just physiological, occurs to your clever little mind!'

'Cause such as glandular fever?'

'Not in this case, though it's a diagnosis I've heard dismissed as bloody-mindedness by the bloody-minded.'

'And one I've known even high-powered and conscientious physicians find difficult to diagnose in the early stages.' I thought Mrs Desmond's secrecy unnecessary, but having promised to maintain it, took refuge in platitudes. 'No matter how pleasing, the marriage of one's only daughter can be a traumatic experience, Australia's a long way off, and commonest things are the most common.'

'And the menopause is a difficult time for women and I've an Oedipus! What's your other little problem?'

I didn't answer. We drove out of the village and along the first of the many side lanes that were a short-cut to the motorway in a blazing silence. Being on edge I played with the nearest buckle, a habit my mother said had started in my pram. Suddenly, he drew up in a passing place.

'Why've we stopped?' I demanded more sharply than I could have wished.

He switched off the engine. 'If you haven't seen enough sliced-off faces, I have. You've worked that something strap so slack, first jolt and you'll be out of it and through the windscreen.' He tilted my seat to release the length of strap I had somehow managed to jam underneath. 'Try that for size—and don't be so bloody neurotic, woman!' He brushed my hands aside, then reached forward and opened my door. 'Or get out! Only five miles to Asden and you'll be safer even if these lanes are lonely. Or have you forgotten the high percentage of accidents caused by the driver's mental irritation?'

'No.'

'Then sit still and stop messing about with that bloody buckle! Touch it once more and you walk! And you can stop nerving yourself to repel boarders. All I want right now is to get us both back to London intact.'

I nearly got out, but my feet were hurting. I held my hands in my lap and looked at him. 'This allowed?'

He slammed the door. It was over twenty miles before

94

we spoke again, or far as I knew, looked at each other.

He had avoided the motorway and we were climbing the long, three-lane road running over the Downs. Pre-motorway it had been the main London road, and with the heavy traffic now siphoned off was nearly as quick as the motorway. Once anyone worked in an Accident Unit, fast driving lost its charm. If speed of itself is no killer, accidents at high speeds kill. Nastily.

That bit of road ran up the side of one of the highest hills in the county. It was edged by wide grass verges backed, on our right, by the hill. The far side of the left verge was fenced for its entire length by sturdy iron railings. A few yards from these, the hill fell sharply for hundreds of feet. The view was a local 'must' for tourists.

Spread out below and reaching to the horizon were miles of apple and cherry orchards, deep green hop gardens, acres of yellow corn. The black and white wood-work of the half-timbered farms and one-time yeomen's houses took on a pristine freshness in the evening sun. The pink-fawn bricks of the houses glowed a soft orange and the cottages really did have roses growing round their doors. The cottage gardens were tiny, patchwork quilts, and the printed cones of the white oasts dotted the land-scape like pepper-pots. It was the England of U.S. travel posters and the fact that it actually existed and belonged to me—along with fifty-five million others—suddenly gave me such unexpected and unashamedly possessive pleasure that I regretted our row still more. I wanted to share it with Joss and to tell him I had just belatedly understood something my father once said. In the last war he had been an RAF M.O. He had said that while convinced the outcome of the Battle of Britain would have been the same had it been fought over any other part of the country, he had always thought the Germans had loaded the dice against themselves by attacking over one of the loveliest corners of England. 'No man fights harder,' he said, 'than the man defending his own backyard. That summer the Garden of England was living up to its name.'

Joss's urgent, 'Christ! Watch it, mate!' jerked me back to the present. I looked round and did a double-take.

A large silver car had come round the curve of the hill and was swaying drunkenly from one lane to another. 'Driver had a blackout? Or steering gone, Joss?'

'Seems to be trying to get it under control—' he steered us onto the left verge and stopped. 'He's trying to get it into the hill—oh God!'

The car had hit and reared up the side of the hill. Momentarily it had stayed poised on the two back wheels, then it did a complete backwards somersault. Now, on four wheels but facing uphill, it shot sideways right over the road and grass, then swivelled leftwards and bonnet first pitched into the rails.

I closed my eyes just before the ghastly clatter of metal on metal. 'Joss, has it gone over?'

'No.' He drove on with his foot right down then braked so abruptly only our belts held us in our seats. 'Three inside.' He lunged into the back for his medical bag and ran for the wrecked car. I tore after him. I was dimly aware a white mini had drawn up behind us but on oath couldn't have said who was in it.

The crumpled bonnet was jammed by bent but unbroken railings. The car roof was dented and crinkled as screwed up silver paper. Every inch of glass was opaque but apparently unsplintered. The engine was dead. The smell of leaking petrol was nauseating.

The right hand doors were either locked or jammed, and so was the left rear door. The front opened. Joss was lifting out a girl as I joined him. A youngish man was slumped over the wheel and an old man with white hair was in a heap on the floor at the back.

The girl's eyes were open and had the glaze of acute shock, but otherwise she seemed unhurt. When Joss set her on her feet, she stood unaided. 'She shouldn't walk.' muttered Joss, 'but she's got to get the hell out of here. Take her. I'll get the others.' He dried his hands on the seat of his pants and dived inside.

His hands and the girl were drenched in petrol. She was tallish and fairly slim, but too stunned to move herself. 'Never mind, duckie,' I said, 'I'll carry you.' I hadn't used a fireman's lift since I was a child. She was heavy, but it was easier than I expected.

Joss had laid the old man on the opposite grass verge before I got there. 'Stay with 'em. I'll get the driver.' He vanished again.

I was straightening from depositing the girl, when an elderly lady suddenly appeared from nowhere beside me. She held two rugs. 'Will these help?' she asked unsteadily.

'Thanks.' I covered both figures. 'Were you in the mini? Where's it gone?'

'My husband's gone for help—I insisted—he's nearly eighty—can I help?'

'Could you hold the girl's hand? She's conscious—and for God's sake, don't smoke! Spilt petrol.' I ran back across the road.

Joss had the driver's head and shoulders out. He was roughly Peter's size, a dead weight, and Joss's face was streaming with sweat. 'I said I'd manage! Get out! That engine smells hotter than hell!'

'Don't be such a ruddy hero!' I grabbed the man's legs. 'I've got him. Move!'

'Why do you have to be such a bloody-minded little bitch?' I didn't answer as I needed my breath.

We had just put down the driver when the old man came round, tried to sit up and fell back with a whimper of pain. As Joss crouched by him, I remembered his medical bag. It was still lying on the grass by the silver car. I had gone before Joss saw me. 'Leave that!' He bellowed. 'Come back!'

I had the case and was running back when, it seemed to me simultaneously, the hill exploded and Joss pulled me down with a rugger tackle. When he hauled us both up, the grass around was on fire, the car was hidden in a sheet of flame, the back of his jacket, hem of my skirt, and some of my hair-ends were singed. The case had been jammed between us when we went down and was intact.

The elderly lady was sitting on the grass looking as stunned as the girl. 'You should've left it—you should've left it—where's my husband—these poor souls need a doctor—oh, dear—I'm too old for this.'

Joss had his jacket off and was kneeling by the old man. I jerked my head his way as I had one hand on the girl's and the other on the driver's pulse. 'He's a doctor.'

She was too shaken to believe me until she saw Joss take his spare stethoscope out of his bag.

The driver looked in his late thirties. He was still unconscious. There was an ugly bump and a quite deep but already clotted gash high on his forehead. I could not find any other visible injuries, but did not attempt to move him at all. His pulse was good. 'Bleeding?' asked Joss without looking round.

I knelt by him. 'No. From his pulse more like concussion than a fracture.'

'Hope you're right. Don't touch him more. Girl?'

'Just shock, I'd say.'

'Uh-huh.' He pulled the wrapping off a syringe. 'This poor old boy's got a bump at the base I don't like. His left tib. and fib.'s snapped and I suspect his femur.' He frowned at the fine-boned too blue face under the heavy white hair. 'His heart isn't liking this at all. I don't like pumping stuff in in the dark, but if the ambulance takes much longer—what do you think?'

I took the old man's pulse. Or rather, I tried to take it. 'Joss, you must. He's going.'

'Yep. I know.' He looked round at the empty road, then

took the necessary phial from his bag. 'Hell of a way from Asden,' he said as he gave the injection.

The old man sighed deeply, once, then again, and then his breathing altered to that deeper rhythm. Joss and I breathed out with our hands on wrists thin as paper. 'That's better, Doctor,' I said, and we both smiled.

The elderly lady was watching. 'He really is a doctor. A real doctor.'

I went back to the other two. 'Yes.'

'And you? Another doctor?'

'Trained nurse.'

The girl had opened her eyes again. She had short, thick, light brown hair and a sensible face. I explained for the third time what was happening. This time she understood and tried to smile. 'Thank you,' she whispered.

The driver had not stirred and his heart was magnificent. I returned to Joss and told him.

'That's a break.' He sat back on his heels watching the thin, closed, old face and the slight rise and fall of the rug over the man's chest. He looked very tall and had wide shoulders, but being so thin his body was barely visible under the rug. 'His shape's helping him, but his age isn't.' Joss looked at me. His face was filthy and the cleared patches round his eyes and mouth stood out, whitely. 'If he has to hang on much longer without oxygen—' he looked over my head. 'God bless all ambulance crews!'

So many times, so many patients, so many relatives, had said, 'I don't mind telling you, Nurse, when I saw that ambulance draw up outside, I could've wept with relief.' If I hadn't known precisely what they meant before, I did then.

A police car and motor-cyclist arrived with the ambulance. A second police car and the white mini followed a few minutes later.

The elderly lady and her older husband were a Mr and Mrs Frayling and lived in Asden. They sat together on

99

the grass watching the stretchers being lifted out and into the ambulances. They did not talk. They just watched.

Joss beckoned me from the ambulance. He was going with them to Asden General Hospital. 'You'll bring the car for me?'

'Sure.'

The policeman who had taken our names and addresses came up to say they would be in touch with Joss later about his statement.

'Right. Cathy—'

'Yes?'

'Don't push the car or yourself.' He mopped his forehead with the back of his wrist and left another white streak as the ambulance man shut the doors.

I watched it disappear, then looked over at the still smouldering wreck. And then I had to sit down, fast.

Chapter Eight

The occupants of the silver car were Norwegian tourists. The old man was a retired marine biologist, a Professor Ulvik. The girl was his daughter, Nina, the driver her husband, Arne Alesund. They all lived in Bergen.

'She'll be out tomorrow.' Joss took the motorway turning from the roundabout. 'Alesund probably in forty-eight hours. He was round before I left. No sign of any fracture in his first pictures.'

'Pity that car hadn't belts on the back seat.'

'Yep. It was the roof that clobbered Alesund.' He shook his head at his thoughts. 'They've got the old boy in their pint-sized I.C. He didn't look too good when they let me look in again on my way out.'

'Think he'll do?'

He shrugged unhappily. 'The Night Super seemed an intelligent and efficient woman. The one registrar apparently running the whole bloody shop tonight seemed to know his stuff, though his English wasn't half as good as the Alesunds'. They've one hundred and ten beds, and according to the Night Super without the 'flu bug hitting them as hard as us, they've a chronic staff shortage. The junior night sister running I.C. impressed me, but she only had a couple of teenage kids to help her. I'm dead sure they'll all do their best, and their best can't be bad as

Asden General has a very good reputation. But as nursing a patient with intensive care takes several pairs of skilled hands, it won't be their fault if sometimes their best just isn't bloody good enough. We think we have staff problems! Huh!' He was silent. Then he said, 'I felt an utter bastard walking out, just now.'

'Joss. You had to.'

'I know my medical something ethics! That doesn't mean I've to love them, or myself!'

I looked at his tense profile. He had had a wash and his hair was neat, but I found his appearance as disturbing as that early morning in the office. The crash had given me more than a physical jolt. 'Go ahead and hate yourself, but don't expect me to join the hate-in.'

We were in the slow lane. He checked in the mirror then slowed more. 'Why the other cheek?'

'I have this weakness for living. If you hadn't flung me clear, quite probably I'd now be dead. And as I doubt I could've lugged those men out alone—and anyway wouldn't have been there alone—but for you, those three'd be dead. Would you fancy ending up burnt to a crisp?'

He shuddered. 'Lay off! My stomach's not strong enough!' He smiled faintly, reluctantly. 'This mean the war's over?'

'Until the next one.'

His smile deepened. 'You had me worried. For an ugly moment I thought I must've clobbered your head when I brought you down. Were you hurt?'

'Don't think so. I don't remember. Hey—something else I've forgotten! Your date!'

'Taken care of. I rang from the hospital. That reminds me—' but he stopped as if he had suddenly decided not to share whatever he had remembered. His 'What did you say the old girl's name was?' was an obvious after-thought.

'Frayling. Husband's a retired bank manager,' I added absently, wondering what he wouldn't tell me.

102

'Retired, where?'

'Asden. She told the cops you ought to get a medal.'

'Not you?'

'Well, yes.'

He was amused. 'This togetherness does something deep down to a guy.' We had gone another five miles in silence before he asked abruptly, 'Do you think he'll do?'

I thought of the old man's face as he lay on the grass after that injection. 'Yes.'

'Why?'

That took more time. He didn't hurry me. 'I don't know. Could be wishful thinking, but I don't think it is. Sort of in my bones. You know?'

'Yes. I hope to God you're right. He looked a nice old boy. At his age, he'd want to die in his own home.'

'How about your bones?'

'Go along with yours, but my judgement doesn't. Only one bright spot there; I know I'm too emotionally involved for a balanced judgement.' He smiled at me as we stopped before another roundabout. 'You used to call them your inkstinks when you always won pinning on that repulsive pig's tail.'

'By cheating. I used to squint under the blindfold.'

We continued swopping childhood horror-stories till we crossed the river. 'Second or third left from here, Cathy?'

'Third, and last house but one on the right.'

When he drew up, as our relationship had taken a great leap backwards I asked him up for coffee and to meet Roxanne. 'Our landlady doesn't object this side of midnight.'

'So Peter says.' He seemed to be having a problem making up his mind. 'Yes—I'd like to see Roxanne. I gather she's worth looking at. What'll she be doing home on a Saturday night?'

'She has a date with a camera outside the Tate Gallery at six tomorrow morning.'

'That figures.'

'It does?' We were out of the car. 'Hasn't got through to Peter in years.'

'Simple soul, Peter, but a decent bloke.' My real brother couldn't have sounded more fraternal.

'Even Homer sometimes nods. Will Roxanne be entertaining?'

I unlocked the front door. 'Doubt it. Why?'

He closed the door first. 'Just remembered something I've been meaning to tell you all afternoon. The bug's taken a new lease in the Orthopod Unit. The wandering boy's wanted back from tomorrow afternoon. John Carr's staying in the A.U. till Stan Lawson gets back at the end of the week.'

I turned from the stairs and faced him very slowly. 'I've never worked with John Carr.'

He was looking at his feet. 'He was J.A.O. a couple of years back, I think.'

'Yes. Just before I got there. Do you mind?'

He looked up. 'Why should I? I crossed the river to be Hoadley East's registrar.'

'So you did.' I had to look away as he was watching me too closely. 'One of these fine days I may even reach Luke. Let's get on up.' I went ahead up the stairs and quickly. I felt as if I had suddenly lost one of my limbs.

Mr Carr was good at the job and pleasant to work with. I did not suspect till his last night that neither of us had enjoyed the week. 'I never knew how I lasted out as J.A.O., Sister. This factory-belt isn't for me. No time to know the patients, follow them through, even remember their names. I'm not surprised Desmond's pleased as hell to be back amongst his orthopods. I can't imagine how Lawson enjoys it—but even he got pneumonia, and Miss Butler got glandular.' He gave me a clinical glance. 'You going to last? You're looking damned peaky tonight.'

That took care of what remained of my morale. 'Just ready for my long weekend, Mr Carr.'

I rang the Night Super at Asden General again before going off. We were now chums. Professor Ulvik had been moved yesterday to a general ward. Mrs Alesund was staying in an Asden hotel to be near him, and her husband had had to return to his job and the three children they had left with his parents in Norway. 'He's beginning to pick up nicely, but not too nicely.' The Night Super's West Indian voice had an attractive lilt. 'As I've just told Mr Desmond, I think we can all be very pleased with ourselves. He is seventy-six.'

I thought of ringing Joss, thought again, and told Dolly as we locked up. She had heard of the crash from George Charlesworth, before I arrived on duty on Sunday morning. On Tuesday, I had heard from Peter that the police had proved the steering column of the car had snapped before it burnt. On Wednesday, thanks to Mrs Frayling, the Asden Gazette made its weekly appearance with a front-page story that included potted biographies of my father, the Vicar, Joss and myself, and an interview with the head teacher of Asden Grammar School. 'Catherine was a reliable and popular prefect and a valued member of our First Hockey Eleven.'

My copy from Mrs Desmond arrived on Friday. Dave Palmer had one on Thursday from grandparents living near Asden. Had Joss not already made it public property, the grapevine would have had the hottest story in weeks. In the event, aside from being wished a good game of hockey by the A.U. staff every time I went off duty, being old history it caused no comment.

From Dolly and via a friend she had staffing in Florence, the A.U. knew of every visit Joss paid Miss Butler, how often he sent her flowers—and the variety, his choice of soothing books, and the size and price of the boxes of Edinburgh rock on her bedtable, the sweet being one for which she appeared to have an insatiable taste. When Dolly announced Joss was taking her home next weekend before she flew to Malta for a minimum of two months sick leave, Dave Palmer suggested we must, but must, have a whip round for the wedding present. 'And shouldn't we spare a few teensy-weensy new pence towards the wreath for the many ever-so-dear girlish hopes those wedding bells'll kill stone dead? But woe!'

That night, after I had given her the latest on Professor Ulvik, we found Dave's watch on a shelf in the plaster room. George Charlesworth was on call. Dolly said he was bound to waylay her on her way out and she would give him the watch for Dave. 'A nice child, Dave, but it's time he grew up.'

I was curious. 'Why do you say that?'

'Sister, dear Sister! Malta's a long way off. Our Mr D. is dead sexy, dead human and so are les girls.'

I smiled over-brightly. 'You don't reckon much to fidelity!'

'No.' Her smooth, chubby, dolly-face both hardened and saddened. 'Nor would you, if your dad had walked out on your mum when you were seven, just because the child he'd given her turned out to be a hydrocephalic.'

We were alone in the department. I leant against the plaster table, appalled. 'Dolly, I didn't know—'

She shook her head, but she didn't hear me. She stared at the blank X-ray screen and the pictures she saw evoked a blazing bitterness in her huge eyes. 'He was a cute baby. He smiled and smiled, but he could never sit up. He died when he was three. My mum's never got over him, or my father. She's loved the selfish sod. God knows how—but women are such bloody fools!' She paused and I kept quiet, partly as I was too moved, partly as she needed to say more. 'Women are so brainwashed into a fear of insecurity, they swallow all that blurb about love and marriage being the only answer, whole. Then they discover marriage is the second biggest con-trick ever pulled on women. Maternity has first place.' She faced me. 'My mum was twenty-seven when she was lumbered with the baby and me. She'd no training and couldn't leave us to get one. Dear old dad paid maintenance just often enough to keep him out of jug. Not that mum would've put him there. I would! She's forty-two now and looks sixty.'

'Dolly,' I said, 'to say I'm sorry is almost an insult. I just wish I'd known—'

'Apart from Miss Evans, you're only the second person I've told in Martha's. The other—guess who—' she smiled very faintly '—our Mr D. My father rang one night we were doing notes late. The switchboard meant to be helpful and put him through. He started creating when I wouldn't talk to him. Mr D. fixed him. I'd had to tell him a little. Then I told him the lot. He was perfectly sweet. Know what he said?'

'Tell me.'

She blushed. 'This'll sound rather awful, but he said he thought this probably explained why I was such an out-standingly good accident nurse.'

'I think he's right on both counts.' I was nearly as appalled by my own blindness. Neither in Albert nor here had it ever struck me she had one serious personal problem. 'I'll tell you something I shouldn't. Miss Evans and Miss Mackenzie want you in Butler's job when she finishes her contract. Like it?'

Her face lit up. 'Give my soul for it!' The light went out. 'Think Mr D.'ll have told Butler? Men blab worse than girls when they think they're in love. George tells me everything—silly yobbo!'

'I don't think Joss will.' I reminded her how long I had known him. 'Even as a boy he knew how to keep his mouth shut and all the Desmonds have a very kind streak. Incidentally,' I added slowly, 'so has George

Charlesworth. He's a gentle, steady lad. I now understand you're dead scared of getting involved, but do me a favour. Give him—and yourself—time. Just time. Don't push him out of your life too fast. Take ten years. I'll bet George is still waiting.'

She said simply, 'Duckie, I hope not. I like George, and it won't do him any good with me.'

I was uncomfortably certain she was right.

Peter was waiting to drive me home. He was annoyed by my delay, peeved to hear Roxanne was in Portugal with her father, as it was a place he had always wanted to visit and could never afford. I was relieved when he decided not to come up for coffee. It had been a heavy day and Peter's bleatings after the patients' and Dolly's genuine problems had irritated instead of mildly amusing me. When I let myself in to our flat I was glad to be alone with my thoughts. Then I started thinking. That was not my favourite night of the year.

Mrs Desmond came up to see Dr Lincoln Browne on the following Wednesday afternoon. She arrived nearly as apprehensive about meeting Joss as about her check-up. 'How can you be so sure we won't run into him, dear?'

I explained Sir Hoadley had started his Wednesday theatre list at one p.m. for the last twenty years. It was then two. 'They're doing eleven this afternoon. The first two are bone-grafts and'll take hours. They'll be in the theatre till nearly seven.'

'Eleven operations? In one afternoon?'

The number wasn't exceptional, but to soothe her I blamed the heatwave.

She turned into an elderly woman when the consultant's secretary ushered her in. Half an hour later she had shed twenty years. 'Darling, such a relief! He wired me up to his machine, showed me the graph I didn't understand at all, but he says my heart is splendid! Can I take you out to tea?'

Being due back in the A.U. in forty minutes, I took her to the Sisters' dining-room. 'Don't worry. Even if the orthopaedic theatre goes mad and stops work, Joss won't come in here. Our residents need a gun at their heads to come through that door.'

Mrs Desmond glanced at the few, mostly elderly Home Sisters, delicately consuming cucumber sandwiches at Miss Evans' table. Miss Evans was not present. The Sisters were not talking and from the gravity of their expressions had unanimously agreed a little nourishment was in order as one always had to wait the hour before performing Last Offices.

'Not that I'd mind seeing Joss now—' Mrs Desmond hushed her voice in sympathy, 'but he might. Even one's unpossessive children can be extraordinarily so, at times. And no matter how well one knows them—or thinks one does—one can never be quite sure what will hurt them and what won't—or I can't. So, as that nice man says no one has to be told anything, can we leave it between us? And, dearie, do advise me further. I'm sure I should pay someone something. His secretary said, no. Yet he saw me as a private patient!'

'No. As the mother of one of the staff. Some of our pundits might have charged you. Not Lincoln Browne. It's an old Martha's tradition that the hospital looks after its own and he's nuts on traditions. Wasn't this so at Benedict's?'

'Mercifully, I never had occasion to find out. Can I write and thank him?'

'Probably make his week if you do.'

She was puzzled. 'Patients don't thank specialists?'

'Generally,' I said, 'and oddly, only when everything's gone wrong. Then the pundits are inundated with letters from grateful relatives.'

'Now I come to think of it, Joss once said that!' She adjusted the set of her small (for her) cream boater. 'I suppose you don't see so much of him, now?'

I had not seen him since the night he left our flat. 'Martha's is a big place.'

The temperature went on rising. Saturday was the hottest day in London since the summer of '59. That evening the flags on our terrace were still steaming, little bubbles of liquid tar were dotting the hospital yard, and the oil from the turning and parked ambulances gave it a surface like ice.

The A.U. was air-conditioned, but all day every cubicle, every bed, had been re-occupied as soon as it was emptied. It was well after ten when Stan Lawson limped into my office, flopped onto one chair, arranged another for his feet, and pushed his glasses up on his high forehead. 'Cath,' he said, 'I know just how Canute felt. But he only had to deal with a mighty ocean of water.' His long, thin, humorous face was made longer by the very short hair-cut he had acquired since we last worked together. Other-wise, we had picked up where we left off. 'This is one of those times when I despair for the human race. When they aren't trying to kill each other on the roads, they're on the job with broken bottles, knives, razors, chair-legs. How many fights in so far?'

'Twenty-one.'

'Forty, last night. At this going we'll top that by midnight.'

Peter had come in. He sat on a hard chair against the wall, leant back and closed his eyes. 'Why can't the sods live in peace?'

'We'd be out of a job Friday and Saturday nights if they did.' Stan loosened his tie, uncapped his pen. 'Cath, remind me to write the brewers a note of thanks for keeping us off the dole queues.' He read my first entry in the log. 'Sylvia Mary Eccles, Mrs, 34 C. of E. What in the name of God did I do for Sylvia Mary?'

I passed him her accident card. 'You told Mr Palmer to put five stitches in her left wrist.'

'So I did! The cat jumped in from the garden, knocked the empty milk bottles into the sink, bust half the breakfast china and what her hubby said she wouldn't like to tell me, doctor, she was sure. Sylvia Mary was damned lucky.' He wrote as he spoke. 'Another millimetre and she'd have sliced her radial artery—and what would hubby have said then? Damned lucky to have a garden, this weather. Wish I had one.'

I said, 'I didn't know you liked gardening.'

'Detest it! But if I had a garden I'd have a lawn. Then I could paddle my poor feet in the early morning dew.' He glanced at Peter. 'He asleep?'

'I think so. Peter?' Peter didn't react. 'Flat out.'

'Some people have it easy.' He wrote on. 'Did I tell you I ran into Desmond and Miss Butler leaving for the country after lunch? She looks a new girl. Wouldn't mind being down in Kent with them tonight.'

'Should be cooler there. Ready to sign?' The red light was flashing. 'Oh, no!'

He took the red receiver from me. 'You, Sister, are off! Unless this is a major, it's going to Emergencies.'

I still heard Harry, the senior night porter, clearly. 'Got a kicks in the face coming in for you, Mr Lawson. Male. Young. Five teeth gone. Query fractured jaw. What do you want me to do with him when he arrives?'

'Harry, Sister is present so I will refrain from specifying more than—keep him in Emergencies. I'll be in.'

Peter had woken. 'God, how I hate Saturday nights!'

I said, 'This heat can't last.'

'Nothing,' said Stan, 'ever lasts. It may look that way, but in this life, my friends, it doesn't. Not even these notes, Cath. We'll finish 'em by midnight—if we're bloody lucky.'

It was exactly midnight when Harry got me a taxi. The taximan said, 'Working the late shift, eh?'

I didn't tell him the truth as he wouldn't believe it. I

didn't hold that against him as there were some truths I did not want to face, myself. 'Yes. Happens, sometimes.'

Chapter Nine

Roxanne was back from Portugal and spent three days modelling furs. By the third evening she looked as if she had been put through a mangle. 'Those lights in this heat! If any man offers me a mink after this, I'll strangle him with it!'

'I wouldn't.' I kicked off my shoes, hung my legs over the arm of a chair and closed my eyes. 'I'd flog it and use the lolly on getting this flat air-conditioned.' I opened one eye. 'I thought there was some knees-up your agent said you mustn't miss tonight?'

'That's tomorrow. Got a light?'

I chucked her matches. 'Who're you going with?'

'Joe.'

'Doesn't he always end up sloshed blind?'

'Yes, but he can be darned amusing till he passes out, so long as he keeps off the subject of his ex-wife. He knows I'll take myself home when I've had enough. And drunk or sober,' she added, 'he's a very good photographer.'

There was a tremendous thunderstorm during the following afternoon. The A.U. had its quietest evening in weeks. Stan and I had finished the notes and were doing a newspaper crossword, when Peter put his head round the door and said he'd drive me home for a cup of Roxanne's coffee. She made superb coffee.

I explained why she would be out. 'Lift off?'

'Don't be so bloody silly! Of course not!' He stomped on down the corridor.

Stan glanced up. 'What's got him?'

I shrugged. 'Storm's still in the air. I'm surprised more people haven't been edgy during this heat.'

'I'm not. To be edgy, one needs time in which to feel hard-done-by. No time, no edges, and no insomnia. Been sleeping like a log?' I nodded. 'Same here and I'll bet throughout the A.U.' He filled in another word. 'Finland—and it fits. Didn't Peter go there last year?'

'Forgotten—no—yes—he sent me a postcard.'

'Time he had another holiday. He got one fixed up?'

'Dunno. What's a voracious sea-bird? Nine, down.'

He blinked at me owlishly, a sign his quick brain was in action. 'Cormorant.' He reached for the green receiver as the green light flashed. 'Probably me.'

It was. He wrote in 'cormorant' as he listened to a long spiel from Harry. 'I'll bet she is. Right, I'll be in, now.' He stood up, smiling. 'We do get 'em!'

Two foreign seamen, each with a black eye, had walked unannounced into Emergencies and sat themselves in wheelchairs. 'Seems they don't understand English, Spanish, Maltese, Italian, French, German, or Polish. Harry's been rounding up night orderlies as interpreters and the Night Super is out for his blood.'

I smiled. 'You off to transfuse him?'

'Harry'll survive, but he's not so sure about his young ladies. He's got them lads under his eye, Mr Lawson, sir, as he doesn't reckon much to the looks they're giving his nurses and though that young Mr Smith's doing his best, he's only a slip of a lad as don't need a shave more than once a fortnight and he reckons the senior night staff nurse is a bit worried, like. And seeing we're quiet and

114

I'm a married man, meself, he thought, did Harry, he'd best have a word with me.' He polished and replaced his glasses. 'Forgive me if I go and prevent multiple rape?'

'Any time. Stan, might they be Norwegians?'

He blinked again. 'That's a thought.'

Peter was delighted Stan thought he needed a holiday. 'Understanding chap, Stan. Sensitive.'

'He should've been a physician.'

'Come off it, Cath! All surgeons may just be bloody technicians but that doesn't make them all insensitive butchers.'

I allowed he had a point and did not pursue mine as there were some things I preferred to keep to myself. I had been back long enough to realise Roxanne had been right about Peter. Even if he still bleated, he had grown up. He had never had, and probably never would have, Stan and Joss's intuitive faculty of perception, but once he caught on he considered every facet of a situation with the plodding thoroughness that solves difficult diagnoses and great crimes. He was mildly enjoying anaesthetics, if not enough to want to specialize. Latterly, he had begun speculating about general practice. I told him I thought this the best idea he had ever had. Despite his occasional conviction he was unloved and unwanted, he was one of the few people I knew whom everyone liked. My father thought it more important for a G.P. to like, and be liked, by humanity, than to have a burning zeal to heal. 'The most useful qualities are stamina and patience. If he's got patience, his practice'll flourish and his patients forgive him any number of mistaken diagnoses. Nine out of ten patients don't come to surgery for a diagnosis, they come because they've got to talk to someone, or crack. Mind you, if you don't listen, back they come with their ulcers, dermatitis, asthma, urticaria—the lot!' Peter was normally very patient, which was why he had just surprised Stan. His constitution was as strong as his build. I

115

now thought him made for a G.P., though before I went to Canada I would have said he was far too immature. Recently, I had realized that could merely have been because the same applied to myself.

He was making coffee and I was doing my hair when Stan rang to ask if Peter had a Finnish phrase book. 'We've decided our lecherous, black-eyed mariners may be Finns. If he can't oblige, ask if he knows a good Finnish brush-off. The night staff nurse—and Harry—are on the verge of acute anxiety states.'

I called Peter. 'Stan wants some Finnish four-letter words.'

'Stan wants—what?' Peter charged in pushing his hand through his hair. Stan's comments made him flop backwards onto my bed and shout with laughter. 'Yes. In my room. Help yourself.' He rang off and smiled up at me. 'How much of that did you get?'

'Only your bawdy splutters.'

'Just as well, when Stan's on form.' He undid his tie. 'That storm hasn't made it any cooler.'

'Still hanging around.' My shoes were full of feet so I removed them. 'I've never heard Stan on form.'

'Nor will you.' He stretched out his arms, contentedly. 'Take more than Women's Lib to crack our Stanley's solid non-conformist upbringing.' He raised his head. 'Isn't that your living-room door?'

I went out to investigate and forgot the comb in my hand till the sight of Joss following Roxanne in made me drop it. 'Hi!' I said weakly, and ran out of conversation.

Joss was in a dinner-jacket that had been cut by a good London tailor this year. Roxanne's long blue-grey printed voile was edged with layers of lace. The dress had a very high lace collar, long graceful sleeves and could have been worn by her great-grandmother, had the skirt in front not been split from hem to thigh. The opening was edged with more lace and her tights matched the blue in the

116

material. They could both have stepped out of one of Roxanne's magazine photographs. I felt like Little Orphan Annie after a particularly tough stint with my begging bowl.

Roxanne was explaining her joy at recognizing a human face at the worst party of the year, when Peter ambled through my bedroom door slowly replacing his tie. Roxanne stopped in mid-sentence. 'Didn't see your car, Peter!'

Peter exchanged amiable waves with Joss. 'Had to leave it round the corner. Joss rescued you from a fate worse than death? Bad champagne?' He was watching her with such open hostility that I almost forgot Joss was watching us both. 'How come you were there, Joss?'

'I've been dining with my old boss from Benedict's. He had to look in and asked me along to give him an excuse to get away, fast. I introduced him to Roxanne.' He smiled at her. 'That's taken care of my next job.'

Roxanne blew him a kiss. 'Why don't we all have a drink?'

Joss said if it was all the same to her after all the bad champagne he'd as soon have some of the coffee they had just turned off.

'My coffee!' Peter slapped his forehead. 'Had it boiled over?'

'The plate was red-hot.' From Roxanne's tone, Peter was clearly trying to bankrupt us through our electricity bills and, failing that, to burn the house down. 'I suppose we should be thankful it wasn't gas.'

'Oh, I don't know,' said Joss. 'Isn't gas cheaper?'

I was about to explain Stan's call, but Peter had caught my eye. 'If it had been gas,' he remarked with uncharacteristic smoothness, 'what a wonderful way to go.'

I thought of Dolly Jones for several reasons. 'Let's all have some coffee.'

Roxanne and Joss sat entwined on the sofa. Peter sat

117

on the arm of my chair and when not playing with my hair, dutifully nibbled my ear. As Roxanne always looked especially good when she was angry and had to hide it, the only person I wasn't sorry for was Joss. The atmosphere reminded me very much of my first week in the A.U.

It eased, briefly, when Joss said he had seen Professor Ulvik and Mrs Alesund in Asden last weekend. The Professor's slow progress was continuing and his daughter had asked for my private address. 'She wants to see you again. All right my handing it out?'

'Sure.'

Peter slid into the chair behind me, lifted me onto his lap and wrapped his arms round my waist. 'Much more comfortable,' he murmured as if we were alone.

Roxanne ignored us and nibbled Joss's ear. I asked if the Norwegians intended claiming damages from the hire-car firm. Joss shook his head, which couldn't have been easy as Roxanne had very good teeth.

'Why not?' demanded Peter. 'Surely, the firm'll be only too happy to settle out of court?'

'They've offered. The Alesunds won't touch it. She said her father'd blow all fuses at the mere suggestion, and they think he's right.' He was suddenly embarrassed. 'They think they owe England too much.'

'Good God! Why?' Peter, Roxanne and I spoke together.

'Something to do with the last World War.' He looked directly at me for the first time since he came in. 'Seems they've long memories in Norway.'

'Rule Britannia.' I met his eyes and nearly said that again when he had to look away first.

But for our landlady's rule we would probably have sat there all night as very obviously neither man intended making the first move. At two minutes to twelve, Joss kissed Roxanne and Peter kissed me. They went down the top flight side by side and looking straight ahead.

118

I closed the door and leant against it. 'If there's one thing I enjoy, it's a jolly evening with chums.'

Roxanne was stretched on the sofa with her eyes shut. 'Cathy, I'm terribly sorry. Just because my party was a drag was no reason for busting up yours—'

'Don't be a moron, Roxanne—'

'Don't be so bloody charitable!' She sat up. 'Think I don't know why Peter was in such a filthy temper when we walked in? Think Joss didn't catch on? Long before Peter spelt it out?'

I said, 'No. We weren't. We haven't. We won't.'

She went scarlet. 'For God's sake! Which century do you think I'm living in?'

I had never known her so angry. I was so fascinated, I forgot my own. 'I'll tell you what you interrupted—'

'Thanks, but I can go to an X movie—'

'This one kicks off with two Finnish sex-maniacs in wheelchairs—' I smiled at her expression. 'True. Listen.' And when I finished, 'Don't ask me why Peter took your turning up with Joss as a slur to his virility. Could be Joss makes him feel inferior, but I'm not asking. I like my beautiful relationship with Peter and asking dodgy questions is the second best way of killing any beautiful relationship stone cold dead. Do you want the bath first?'

'No.' She had stopped looking angry and in self-defence had fallen into one of her professional poses. We privately called this one 'Nobody knows the trouble I've seen but stick around, buster, and you'll find out.' I did not say so, now. 'Cathy—'

'Yes?'

'This—umm—Martha's Foundation Ball in September. Hasn't Peter asked you?'

'Yes. Joss—you?'

'Yes. When he drove me back. Think we'll—umm—join up?'

'And which century do you think you're living in, Roxanne?'

119

I did not discuss that evening with her again, or with Peter in the A.U. It was getting on for three weeks before I next saw Joss and by then I had other things on my mind.

The temperature had returned to normal for late summer and as August ended our admission rate rose to its normal Bank Holiday climax. In one of the three momentary lulls we had that Monday, Dave Palmer said he didn't think he would ever be able to eat food his hands had touched again. 'But useless, utterly useless, to tell me I've been wearing gloves. They reek of blood, positively reek!' He groaned at another red flash. 'Dear lemmings. Go home.'

'Brace up, lad,' said Stan. 'Holocaust season closes after today till Christmas. Well, Sister?'

I read aloud Nurse Hedges' memo sheet. 'Six. Two adults, four children. One family. Estate car . . .'

Five minutes later Hedges was back. 'Both sets of parents of that honeymoon couple are here, Sister.'

'Waiting-room and tea, Nurse. Mr Lawson'll see them soon as he's free.'

Another memo sheet. 'Elderly pedestrian. Male. Knocked down by van. Multiple injuries. Name, address, unknown.'

Message after message. Accident-trolley after accident-trolley. The same anguished mutters, the same whimpers of pain, the same sickly sour smell of fresh-spilled blood. Relative after relative, sitting in rows in our waiting-room in the same incongruously garish holiday clothes, with the same stunned expressions on their faces.

The estate car had belts fitted to the front and back seats. The youngest child had been in a safety-harness and the other three wearing their belts. The parents had left theirs undone. The father had been doing around seventy when he had a front off-side blow-out. Both parents were sent to I.C. on the Dangerously Ill List. The children were shocked and cut by flying glass, but none seriously.

The youngest had come off best as she had been asleep. She was four, very chubby and articulate, and her name was Jeanie. The precautionary X-ray showed her skull to be so perfect and intact that George Charlesworth breathed in sharply as it was illuminated on the X-ray screen. 'My God,' he muttered to Stan. 'Come and look at this.'

Jeanie looked seriously at the two men, then plucked my gown sleeve. 'Is that really him?' she whispered.

I bent over her. 'Sorry, lovey, I don't understand. Really who?'

Her round baby face was alight with excitement. 'God. That tall gentleman with the glasses. That's what the small gentleman with the glasses called him. I didn't know God wore glasses though I know He wears a long white dress as I've seen pictures of him.' Stan had overheard and moved to her other side. 'Please, are you God?'

Stan flushed to the roots of his short hair. 'No, love, sorry. I'm just same as your Daddy, only I'm a doctor. Know what a doctor is?'

'Doctors mend people. Mummy told me.' She gave George Charlesworth an accusing glare. 'Why did that small gentleman with the glasses call you God?'

George Charlesworth was pink. Stan answered for him. 'He wasn't really talking to me, Jeanie. He was—he was sort of saying a little prayer.'

With the total unselfconsciousness of the very young, she flattened her fat little hands together under her chin. 'Like "Gentle Jesus meek and mild"?'

For a moment the two men and I were silent.

'That's right, love,' said Stan. 'Like that.'

On that same table, that morning, the three of us had stood and watched a slightly older child die.

Later, Stan said, 'I wish I could have the buggers here.'

I was punch-drunk from the day. 'Which buggers, Stan?'

'The buggers who were in too much of a hurry to get to the sea—to Auntie May's—to the pub—the best picnic spot. I wish I had them here. And you know what I'd do?' I shook my head at his tired, grim face. 'I'd not take 'em to I.C., the kids' wards, the bloody shambles the girls are now turning back into a clean Receiving Room. I'd not bother showing 'em the relatives, or let 'em listen to that "We never thought this could happen to us, Doctor!" I've had over and over all day. None of that!' His voice shook with the dreadful anger of a peaceable man. 'I'd just take the buggers to the morgue. I'd stand 'em there, a bit, to listen to the ticking of the fridges. Then I'd pull out just the one shelf. The one with that little lad with half his head missing. And I'd say, "Take a look, mates. You've got the time. Saved it on the roads today, didn't you? And this is what those few minutes bloody cost. Take a good look. Then —— *off* home and sleep easy."'

I did not say anything. I left him in the office and went along to the relatives' waiting-room. It had finally emptied, the tea-urn was only lukewarm, but there was enough left for one cup. I took it back, put it by him and sat down again. After he had drunk the tea we did the notes.

Chapter Ten

I had a letter from Mrs Alesund next day and we met for lunch in the following week. She was waiting in the foyer, but I did not immediately recognize her as the young woman in a tan jersey suit and tan velvet beret.

She was amused. 'My face is clean!'

'Mine, too, but you recognized me.'

She had unusually wide-set eyes with an even more unusual quality of innocence in their expression. 'Miss Maitland, Arne and I have three children. Our boy is eight, our girls seven and five. I shall never forget either your face or Mr Desmond's. Now, sherry?' Her fluent English was only slightly accented. 'Or something else?'

I had rather dreaded that lunch, having recently discovered how uncomfortable a burden was gratitude. I was now finding it as hard to dismiss Joss as not worth bothering over, as to meet him without feeling irritated and vaguely guilty, because I probably owed him my life. I had expected much the same reaction to myself from my hostess. It was not all that uncommon in patients after a successful recovery from a dangerous illness. My father had said that was because few people cared to recall their black periods or those connected with them. 'It is so much easier to be a generous giver. To be a generous taker requires real, and rare, generosity of spirit.'

Mrs Alesund possessed it. Her friendliness was uneffusive, but she made it very plain she was my friend for life. She talked as an old friend, of her family, and father. He was now up on crutches and hoping to leave hospital, shortly. 'He's so enjoyed his regular visits from Mr and Mrs Frayling, and the Vicar and Mrs Desmond. With the Vicar he's got on very well as both men are scholars and served in your Royal Navy during the last World War.'

'I knew the Vicar had been a Naval padre.' I did not add that the rest was news to me.

'An interesting and amusing man. Coffee?'

'Thank you.' She had not mentioned Joss again. I did, and learnt he had driven her over to tea at the vicarage on his half-day last week.

'It was a lovely afternoon and we had tea on the lawn. It was a very pleasant and very English occasion.'

'With wasps in the raspberry jam and suicidal flies in your tea?'

She laughed. 'Having lived next door for so long, those wasps will be your old friends. I had hoped young Mr Desmond could join us today, but unfortunately he's working. Of course, you'll know that.'

'No.' I explained our different jobs.

She seemed surprised. 'Not your young man?'

I smiled. 'Boy next door.'

She agreed that was often an insuperable barrier later and asked if I had ever visited Norway. 'You must! It is a beautiful country. Do you ski?'

'I did some in Canada. I loved it, though I'm no good as I started too old. Your children ski?'

'Indeed! Norwegians are on skis as soon as they can walk. You must spend a winter holiday with us sometime. When do you next have a holiday?'

124

I took her invitation as a charming gesture, but not to be taken seriously. 'Thanks, I'd love to.' I went on to tell her my immediate future remained problematical owing to Butler's health. Miss Evans had said I must have two weeks off before the end of the year, possibly late October or early November and would that suit me? Since the last thing I presently wanted was the thinking-time a holiday would provide, I said, very well, thank you. Miss Evans had then given me a long look and asked how many days off I had owing. My answer evoked a deep sigh. 'Not blaming you, my dear. I haven't a sister who escaped the 'flu who doesn't now need a rest-cure. Now, let me see—' she studied a rota. 'Yes. By the last weekend of this month, Nurse Chalmers'll be back—her father's much better—and Nurse Jones from her holiday. Take from Thursday to Tuesday, inclusive.'

Mrs Alesund asked if I would spend my break at the vicarage. I said I thought not as there was so much I wanted to do in London. We agreed London was a fascinating city, though the traffic was terrifying. She was returning to Asden that afternoon and to Norway tomorrow. Before I left, she asked me to call her Nina. 'I think of you as Cathy, having heard your old friends use the name so often. I won't say goodbye, as we will meet again. Till then.'

I wrote that off as another charming gesture. I said as much to Joss when I met him by chance on my nightly visit to the Office with the A.U. report that evening. He was in a hurry, too. He said I could be right, that he had been sorry to miss our lunch but I knew how it was. I said I did and we went our separate ways. When I looked back he had disappeared.

'You're very grave, Sister. Disturbing evening?'

'Er—no, Miss Evans. Quite quiet.'

Back in the Receiving Room, one of the medic. students was trying to unload the last four unsold ball tickets in his book. 'Best knees-up of the year status-wise! Come on, Mr Lawson! Make the in scene!'

'Dance, lad? Me? When I've flat feet and am tone deaf? What are you trying to do? Deprive me at a stroke of my job and my lovely wife? Take a look at next week's off-duty rota on that board! Mr Charlesworth's just told you he's got his tickets. How long'd I draw my pay if I left the shop to run itself? And how'd I persuade my wife not to fulfil her promise to divorce me if I risk crippling her on a dance floor the once more? Away, wretched youth! Flog 'em elsewhere!' He glanced at the lights. 'Thought this peace was too good. And the next one is—Sister?'

Nurse Black was 'lights and messages.' We were patientless, so she read aloud: Youth, name, address, unknown. Minor burns, shock, semi-drowned. Clothes set alight when removing paint from house-boat with blow-lamp. Jumped in river, can't swim. River police witnessed event, bringing him in.'

'Makes a change.' Stan washed his hands. 'If there's one thing I like, it's a bit of variety.'

Peter waved off the ticket-seller like a fly. 'If you ask me, the chap was flogging tickets. My blow-lamp still handy, Sister?'

'On the anaesthetic machine in C2, Dr Anthony.' There was a roar of laughter as the medic in question glanced into C2 instinctively. 'It's all right, Mr Dennis. Dr Anthony only chucks medics in the river when there's no R in the month.'

'Only snag there, I can never remember the date.' Peter smiled at me over his mask as the red light reappeared. 'We're in business again.'

The youth was a Barry Steven Thomas. He was twenty, very skinny, with long, dank, dark hair and a sharp-featured, intelligent face. He worked in a television-cum-radio shop and though semi-conscious on admission, responded so well that initially he refused to be admitted to a ward.

126

'Only got me clobber burnt and a bit of a soaking, didn't I, then? Said yourselves I been dead lucky only to get them small burns. You've fixed me. I'm not stopping.'

Stan had called in a thoracic registrar as some water had penetrated Barry's lungs. The registrar said we'd feel much happier if he would come in for a day or two. 'The Thames isn't precisely crystal clear.'

'Can't be that mucky, Doc, seeing as the fish come back.'

I said, 'You just don't fancy hospitals, Barry?'

'S'not that, darlin'.' He grimaced to himself. 'I'm not fussy, but it's this bird, see? Always meet her down the disco Wednesdays, don't I? Go right spare she will, if she reckons I've turned her in. Have to get meself a new bird, won't I? Don't want no new bird. Proper little darlin', she is. I'm getting out of here, see?'

I said, 'Wouldn't your bird understand if we got a message to her? What's her name? And the disco? Better still, know the number?'

He gave all three. Peter joined us as I was noting the lot on the upturned hem of my gown. Barry said I'd best ask for Big Sid. 'He's all right, is Big Sid. He'll not reckon her name, just say as she's the small blonde job, third table back, right. He'll fetch her, you tell her and I'll sign in.' He winked at the two men. 'Sister's a proper little darlin', ain't she, then?'

Joss stopped by my table in the canteen next day. Peter was in the queue for our coffee. Joss had had a letter from Ruth and she sent me her love. 'She feels marriage is an institution with a great future.'

'I've heard it well spoken of.'

His smile wasn't fraternal, it was downright avuncular. 'Hence the successful Lonely Hearts' Bureau Doug Pearson says you're running in the A.U.?'

Doug was the thoracic registrar. 'All part of the N.H.S.' Since we were so nauseatingly chummy, I asked about the holiday he was starting some time next week. 'Foreign parts?'

127

'I think so, though it's not quite settled.' He looked ostentatiously at the canteen clock as Peter approached with two cups of coffee. 'If that's right, I'm late. Hi, Pete—see you, Cathy!'

Roxanne was booked to make a television commercial in Venice two days after the ball. At the moment, she was doing so well professionally that we barely saw each other. 'Always the same,' she said. 'Either every fashion editor in London wants you at once, or no one remembers your name.'

She was reorganizing the two-foot-long carpet-bag she used for her modelling gear some nights later when I got back by taxi at eleven. 'Peter on call?'

'No. Something late he wanted to see on telly.' I sat on her bed. 'Where's tomorrow's?'

'Brighton, at eight-thirty.' She muttered to herself as she repacked. 'Shoes—light—dark—high—flat—boots—where the hell are my boots?' I picked them off the floor. 'Thanks. Joss rang me just now to fix up times for Friday. Going to Malta, he said. Isn't that where his regular woman is?'

'Yes. What about sandals?'

'God, yes!' She dived into her shoe-rack. 'Tights. Tights —plain—coloured—body stockings—socks—strapless bras —bra slips—' she looked up. 'These taxis must be costing you a fortune.'

'They are. If you keep on working at this rate, I shall end up bankrupt.'

'Thought you said he was watching telly?'

'Every man needs a hobby, dear.'

She smiled slightly as she intoned over her hair accessories. 'Wigs—hair pieces—heated rollers—spray—where's my blasted setting lotion?' I was sitting on it. 'The client wants a simple day dress, possibly striped. I've got in one striped horizontal, one vertical, one floral, three plain coloureds. Think that's enough?'

'I'd say.' I waited a moment. 'Did you know you make him feel inferior?'

128

'Me *and* Joss?'

'Yes. In different ways.'

She flung herself into the pose we called 'One step nearer, Mr Hands, and I'll blow your brains out.' 'He knows there's a difference?'

I said soberly, 'I think he's serious, Roxanne. I've never thought so before, but I do now. Of course, I could be wrong.' She said nothing. 'Decided you're not interested?'

'Decided I need time to think. I was so sure eventually you two would drift into marriage. I can now see that's not on, but—' she zipped up the bag '—nor is my chucking away good lolly I can only earn for a year or two more, to boost any man's ego. And even when the public get sick of my face, as they will, I'll never settle for being the doctor's wife. I'll turn agent and I'll make a lot of lolly. I like lolly and I like working. How about his ego, then?'

I thought it over and had to be honest. 'I think it might work providing you were hellish tactful. Is he worth it, to you?'

'I don't know. I've got to think.'

I said, 'He's only soft-centred. He's not all mushy.'

'I like soft-centres.' She lit a cigarette. 'I'm just not sure the time's right. My dad says everything depends on timing. He says if you can get your timing right, you can be the biggest ham in the business and still have 'em queueing in the rain for a mid-week matinee in Wigan. Get it wrong, and no matter how talented, you'll lay an egg. He says it's the same off-stage, and that lots of people mess up their opportunities not because they don't recognize 'em, but because they grab 'em at the wrong moment.' She gazed at the bag. 'Maybe I should take the dog-tooth check. Yes. I will.'

She was still dressing when Peter came for me on Friday night. We didn't wait as we were joining separate parties, if for no other reason than convention. The tables round the floor always were booked months in advance by the various Units. Comparatively, the A.U. staff was small and we had a single table for six. The Orthopaedic Unit needed two tables pushed together and fourteen chairs. Being the social event of the hospital year, the residents always drew lots before buying tickets. The losers stayed on either in their own jobs, or on loan. Stan had kept out of the draw, which automatically freed George Charlesworth. He was with Dolly, and Dave Palmer, smirking with his luck in the draw, had brought the very pretty Nurse Fisher.

Stan was running the A.U. with Hamish Geddes, a locum anaesthetist from Swansea, and Mr Smith from Emergencies. Stan sent us a message on a memo sheet via one of Harry's night porters. 'Minorities appeased. Smith's home, Ulster. Have requested precautionary peace-keeping force from U.N. Enjoy *dolce vita*, but kindly refrain from bringing pieces for repair to A.U. as scuppers already awash with blood and beer from regular customers.'

The lace frills on Dave's shirt provided universal joy and attention until Joss walked in with Roxanne. Her tight-fitting, apparently seamless, sleeveless black velvet dress had a high halter neckline and was split up the left side to mid-thigh. She wore no jewellery and had taken off her watch. The effect hit Peter, as well as every other woman in the room, like a bomb.

Dolly said without rancour, 'I feel like a Christmas tree.'

Peter was breathing carefully. 'That's her job. Have to switch yours, Dolly, if you want to afford fifty quid on a dress.'

I said, 'That dress didn't cost Roxanne fifty quid. Cost her five sixty including the zip. I was there when she bought the material. She made it herself. She likes sewing.'

Fisher was intrigued. 'I've seen her on telly commercials. You actually know her, Sister?'

'Been sharing a flat with her for years.'

'So that's how our dear Mr D. drew the jackpot! Just

because you and he were kiddiwinks together? Why don't any of my dear old kiddiwink chums introduce me to birds that look like that?' Dave was so concerned with his woes he did not notice another houseman removing Fisher until they were on the floor. 'Oh, villainy! I have been robbed—but robbed!'

Peter tritely observed that would teach him a bird in the hand was worth two in the bush—even if poured into black velvet.

George Charlesworth reluctantly took his eyes off Dolly. 'Who's everyone going on about? That bird with Joss Desmond? Oh—yes—not bad. Dance, Dolly?'

Dancing with Peter, I said George revived my faith in human nature. Peter was glad I had any faith left to be revived. 'Let's get some air.'

The ball was in the Medical School's largest ground floor lecture room. The building stood away from the wards and as it was a fine night, all the french windows were open. We went out on the terrace and leant on the stone balustrade overlooking the river. The water was black and smooth as oil. The lights on the embankments and the bridges lined and strung the blackness with yellow diamonds. The empty office blocks on the far bank were towers of white diamonds, and the skyline of the City was charcoal petrified lace against the pink-black London sky.

Peter propped his chin on his hands. 'When I was a student, I thought I'd never be able to leave this. Not that I seriously thought I ever would, if I thought at all. Don't believe I did. I just had a vague idea that if I hung around long enough Membership—,' he smiled at himself, '—and M.D., the lot—would somehow drop into my lap. S.M.O., the Staff, Dr Anthony, sir, Sir Peter Anthony. Lord Anthony. All I needed was patience.'

'Patience you've got, Pete.'

'No. You're mixing it up with laziness. But I don't just want to move off now, as I can't be bothered to make the

131

effort to stay. I now know that if I sweated my guts out, I'd never make the top grade here. Martha's may turn out specialists by the dozen, but I'm not specialist material.' He turned to watch the dancers passing the open windows. 'Not in a million years would it have struck me to risk offending our top brass and getting out of step here, by demonstrating my conviction that some Benedict's man knew more about my line than our own pundits. You don't get to the top without taking chances. I don't like taking chances. Thought I did. I don't.'

I had turned and we were both watching Joss and Roxanne. 'Nor did my father. He loved being a G.P. I think he was a very good one.'

'Joss says he was first-rate.'

'Do you think his gamble'll pay off?'

He nodded gloomily. 'Hoadley's sold on him. Fair enough. He's a bloody good surgeon and he works bloody hard. Everyone at the top in medicine knows everyone else, so they'll have heard across the river. If he'd mucked things up here, Benedict's would never have forgiven him for opting out for Martha's, but if they aren't already cooking the fatted calf, I'll bet it's ordered.' The music stopped. Roxanne, smiling, stretched out both hands to Joss. 'Nothing succeeds like success. Nothing at all.' He swung round to face the water. 'Roxanne's doing very well too, isn't she?'

'Very, though a model's life at the top is generally very short-lived. Have you done anything tangible about G.P.ing?'

'There may be an opening in Leeds in the New Year. A joint practice. Don't suppose I'll get it, but I've applied.'

'Roxanne's home town. You must tell her. She'll be very interested.'

'For God's sake—why?'

'Aren't you interested in anything concerning your own home town? And she may know some of the partners. Her father lives there. I know it's a big city, but most cities break down into villages and everyone in a village knows everyone else's business and more than somewhat about the nearby villages. Got an interview? Then ask her tonight when you dance with her. She's leaving for a job in Venice on Sunday and she might be able to give you some helpful hints if only about which football team not to support.'

He said, 'You're still a lousy liar, Cath. So you think I should dance with her?'

'I'm thinking of Stan. He'll be hellish narked when the river police fish you out of the river.'

He hesitated, then laughed. 'Almost worth it to see Stan's face when they wheel me in. Come on. Let's participate.'

Sir Hoadley was sitting by Roxanne at the O.R. tables when we returned to our own. In common with the many pundits present, he was in tails. Since there was no Accidents' consultant, we all agreed champagne was the only possible antidote to our deprivation symptoms. The popping of Sir Hoadley's shirt-front and the redness of his face provided additional consolation, but we had to avert our eyes from Dr Lincoln Browne. At any Martha's function for the last quarter of a century, the tall, elegant cardiologist had been, and remained, amongst the top three most attractive men present. His grey streaks had altered to white since I last saw him and he had a few more lines and no longer danced since he had had his first coronary. I did not expect him to remember me as it was years since I worked in Cardiacs, but he bowed from across the floor. Dave asked if I shared a flat with him, too?

'Unfortunately, no.'

Miss Evans was impressive in grey lace, Miss Mackenzie terrifying in what appeared to be a black shroud. Sister Florence, the oldest and stoutest sister in the hospital,

133

was draped in purple satin. She loved dancing and stood no nonsense about waiting to be asked. 'Come along, boy! We'll dance!' Having on some occasion in the last twenty years had every member of the nursing staff present as a patient, she toured the tables methodically, checking up on her ex-patients' health, husbands, babies, teenagers' prospects of getting into university, and future nursing careers. 'Can't expect you gals to stay single these days.' She lowered herself into Dave's chair and we all sat down again. 'Too many young men about. First time in history you gals are in a minority group. Enjoying it, eh? Sure you are! I would've loved it!' She peered at Fisher. 'How's that throat, child? Behaving itself? Good. No more trouble with that back, Nurse Jones? Thought it would clear up.' It was my turn. 'No more of that bronchitis you had in your first year? Always said you'd grow out of it.' She noticed Dave's stance. 'Straighten up, boy! Remember your vertebrae! Want a curvature before you're my age?' She suddenly beckoned Joss from the edge of the floor. 'Well, Mr Desmond? Missed you in my ward, lately. Good news from Malta, eh? And who's this pretty gal? Why don't I know you, Nurse? You're not a nurse? Pity. You know how to carry yourself, child. Take my chair—I want a word with Mrs de Winter.' She moved on to the next table.

The second, and olde-tyme group, started up again as I introduced Roxanne to the A.U. party. Joss stood watching in silence with his shoulders back and eyebrows up. Peter dithered until Roxanne smiled straight at him. Two minutes later, Joss and I were alone. He had sat in a chair on the other side of the table before he remembered he was not my brother. 'Or do you feel strong enough for a schmaltzy waltz?'

'My feet,' I said truthfully, 'are killing me.'

He smiled politely. 'Then I can give you the message I should've handed on earlier. Arne Alesund rang me this evening. They've both flown over for a fleeting visit and want us to meet them for lunch up here tomorrow. He rang from Asden.'

'Tomorrow I'm on at one—'

'I said that was on the cards. He suggested coffee, a drink before lunch, or both. Seems they've some specific reason for wanting to see us. Nina would've written you but she's somehow sprained her right hand.'

'I can make anything up to twelve-thirty. How about you?'

He grinned. 'Free man. Holiday started this afternoon.' He stood up as Dr Lincoln Browne was suddenly at my elbow. 'Evening, sir.'

'Good evening, Doctor—and to you, Miss Maitland.' The pundit smiled on us both as he shook my hand. As Joss was a surgeon and had never been one of his students, he obviously did not recognize him. Martha's had roughly ninety residents and even more post-graduates around, and when in doubt all strange men were addressed by the title 'Doctor', and more often than not, correctly.

Dr Lincoln Browne refused a chair as he was leaving and had already said goodnight to Miss Evans. 'Seeing you having this brief rest, I couldn't waste the delightful opportunity. I know you'll be glad to hear I've had a most charming letter from our mutual friend, Mrs Desmond. I was very glad you sent her to me,' he added seriously. 'It's a rare pleasure to be able to remove a genuine anxiety from an intelligent patient. Wish it happened more often. Well! I must just have a final word with my old friend Sister Florence. Very nice to see you back in our midst, Miss Maitland. Goodnight to you both.' He bowed himself off to the next table. Joss bowed back.

I glanced from the next table to Joss. 'Listen—'

'While we indulge in a little therapeutic schmaltz.' He came round and offered his hand. He said nothing until we were dancing. 'Do tell me,' he murmured in my ear, 'to whom have you sent my old man? And Danny? One does rather like to know these things when they concern one's own family.'

My head knocked his chin as I tilted it back to look at his face. 'She didn't want to worry you.'

He gave an equivocal little grimace. 'When did this come up? That Saturday at home?'

'Yes.' I remembered our conversation as we left the vicarage.

So did he. 'Crafty little bitch, aren't you, darling.'

'Joss, I didn't think it necessary—'

'To encourage the lad's Oedipus? Dead right. Can't be too careful with these unnatural emotions. Think where it got Oedipus. Still—thanks.'

I gave up. 'Forget it. Did Arne Alesund give you any idea why they particularly want to see us?'

'He said they'd rather do that *vis-à-vis*. My guess is, they want us to lean on the Prof.' He smiled. 'He's just cracked another new walking-plaster, bouncing on it when no one was looking. His ward sister told me last week she'd be whiter than him before he left. The only way they can get him to rest at all is to hide his crutches. Obviously, takes more than that to restrain the tough old Viking, but he is seventy-six and he has been bloody ill. The Alesunds had hoped to fly him home tomorrow, but he said this afternoon he's quite happy to hang on a few more days and ta-very-much but he hates flying and when he goes home he's going as a good Norwegian should, by sea. And he will—if he doesn't bust his neck testing the next new plaster.'

I was smiling. 'Or telling the Captain how to steer across the North Sea.'

'That's for sure.' He held me closer and we finished the dance in an apparently companionable silence. Being, as we later discovered, the penultimate dance, it was longer than usual. I found it so long I was very glad when it

136

ended. Joss then said he would ring me in the morning after ringing Arne Alesund and took Roxanne back to his own table. Peter collected me.

Next morning Arne Alesund handed me a sherry and Joss a beer. He raised his own beer. 'Skål!' His accent was much stronger and his English less perfect than his wife's. 'Good practice for next weekend, no?'

Joss looked as bemused as I felt. 'Skål!' we said.

Chapter Eleven

The mountains were growing higher and changing colour. They ranged the length of the northern horizon, sepia and charcoal, black and navy blue, all streaked with white and patches of dark green velvet. The long vivid blue slits of the fjords ran softly inwards, like venous blood returning to an invisible, gigantic heart. Beyond the coastal range were more mountains, and beyond those, more mountains, rising up and up to the end of the world. The farthest mountains were half-hidden in mist.

As we sailed closer, the pale grey sea was broken by innumerable rocky islets speckled with moss and scrub bushes and lined with patient rows of sea-birds. The sea was smooth and the morning sun gentle in a cloudless sky.

Joss folded his arms on the rail beside me. 'Pebbles plopped on the water by some absent-minded giant. Incredible,' he mused, 'to think we're so far north in autumn. This could be the Med. in spring.'

'No Force Ten gale,' I murmured, and felt rather than saw him look at me, curiously. Having woken with the type of crashing headache that fills the brain with painful cotton-wool and seals off the world behind a thinner layer, it was some seconds before I recalled never having seen the Mediterranean and tuned in to his train of thought. 'Pity your Malta project had to be cancelled.'

'I'm not all that sold on the sun and I do like Scotland. I hope this weather lasts when I get to Edinburgh next week.'

'This chum Naomi flew back with one of your old chums?'

'Yep. From Benedict's.'

I made no comment partially owing to my headache, partially as I was wondering if he would now tell me Naomi had seen Miss Evans on Wednesday afternoon. When he didn't, I did not tell him I knew she was not returning to Martha's, or that my five days were now tacked on to a two-week holiday. This was our first real conversation alone, since our brief chat over travel arrangements yesterday between Asden station and Asden General. Professor Ulvik had regretted even more volubly than the Alesunds that I was not free to spend longer in Bergen. Since I hadn't known this could be possible till Wednesday night, by which time the Alesunds, at their own expense, had fixed our shipping tickets and the project was already cutting a large enough chunk out of Joss's holiday, it had seemed only tactful to keep it quiet.

I only learnt on the morning after the ball that Joss's previous arrangements had been turned upside down, as Naomi had suddenly decided she wanted to join him in the U.K. Joss said he had already cancelled his flight ticket, but offered no other explanations to the Alesunds or myself. The former had been delighted. 'Speaking frankly,' said Arne, 'we are much pleased and much relieved. The Professor is tall and with his plaster, very heavy. A man is necessary to support and—maybe—keep him a little quiet, no? But Thursday, business forces me to Oslo. I would not be content for Nina, or any other girl, to come with him alone on the sea. Last weekend we had a hurricane. Speaking frankly, next weekend—who knows?'

139

When Joss drove me back to the flat, I said I was surprised Norway sounded as much a man's world as England. 'I thought the Scandinavians were too civilized for that kind of nonsense.'

He frowned at the car ahead. 'Not knowing, can't say. But as the Prof. standing just clears six five, even though he hasn't an ounce of spare flesh, isn't it just possible Arne's argument has a practical rather than prejudiced basis? Almost certainly, you'll outlive me, but the fact remains my muscles are stronger than yours.'

'And trained nurses don't learn how to lift?'

'Cool off, Cathy!' We could have been back in the vicarage schoolroom. 'Only one weekend. They know we're free, we don't want to upset 'em, so we're hooked. As the Chinese so wisely say—relax, and enjoy it!' He drew up and said he would be in touch. He sent me a postcard from the vicarage saying the weather was good, Naomi had guessed the correct weight of the cake at the W.I. 'bring-and-buy', he would meet the 11 a.m. at Asden on Thursday morning and whatever else I forgot, to remember my passport.

Miss Evans had been off duty on Wednesday night. If had been a heavy day in the A.U. Monday and Tuesday had been worse. We now had the full staff back, but when the Office rang to say Miss Evans wanted to see me in her flat, as Miss Evans always did her own dirty work, I was convinced my five days were about to be written off, but was too busy to work out whether I was glad or sorry.

Miss Evans offered me an armchair, a cup of coffee and profound apologies for having to make a request she normally tried to avoid. Then she asked me to add my holiday onto my weekend. 'It won't be too short notice? You're sure? My dear girl, that is a relief! I'll tell you why.'

Naomi Butler had called on her that afternoon and asked to be released from her contract for purely domestic

140

reasons. Miss Evans did not say what these were and etiquette prevented my asking. 'In the circumstances, naturally, I agreed, though I am exceedingly sorry to lose such an excellent nurse. Inevitably, this leaves me with a staff problem and is why I want your holiday over, immediately.' She refilled our cups. 'Nurse Chalmers leaves to marry her parson in November. In December, Nurse White takes her new post in Australia. Had you not already told me you want to return to the wards, I would now be offering you a permanent contract as Sister Accidents. Nurse Jones is not yet sufficiently experienced, but I would say, possibly by January? You agree? Good! So does Miss Mackenzie. And you're willing to remain in the Accident Unit until then? Thank you. Now—what are your views on your present fourth-years?'

Having given them, I said, 'Though still a third, Nurse Fisher is exceptionally good.'

'That pretty little thing? Is she, indeed! I'll bear this in mind when her training ends.' She made a note in the large diary on the coffee table, then glanced up with a wry smile. 'I suppose she's not engaged to young Mr Palmer, as that could be a complication, later. According to Mr Roth, once that young man has his Fellowship, he could make a good future J. and S.A.O. I've nothing against inter-staff—what shall I call 'em?—good friendships, and wouldn't have a hope of stopping them if I had, but I will never knowingly allow an engaged pair, any more than husband and wife, to work in the same department. It isn't fair to impose the inevitable strain on either—and, above all, unless they have rare self-control, it must affect the quality of their work. Consequently, without wishing to pry into my nurses' private lives, I do like to know who is going steady with whom.' My expression amused her. 'Running a large hospital is a complex occupation, and particularly a teaching hospital. The overwhelming majority of my staff are under thirty and—to begin with—single. With our inter-hospital marriage rate, I often wonder if I'm running a hospital or the most successful marriage bureau in London. Do you mind telling me—are those two children thinking of an engagement?'

'Not that I've heard, Miss Evans. I wouldn't even have said they were going steady.' I was fascinated by this latest insight into the life of a high-powered hospital administrator. 'They're both—well—'

'Playing the field?' she queried briskly. 'Good. Good. At their age that's a sign of maturity. I've long observed it's invariably my most immature children who leap into marriage in their first or second years. Sadly, more often than not, inside of five years they want to leap out again. But I've kept you long enough! Enjoy your break, and I have to say, you look ready for it, my dear. Let's hope you return refreshed and not to another 'flu epidemic. Dr Gray tells me the odd case is still appearing around the country.' She saw me to the door. 'I will announce this news after I've spoken to Mr Lawson and Nurse Chalmers over the weekend. For the present—I think we've just decided you need more than a weekend's rest. Have a good time—and thank you very much!'

No one in the A.U. had time to ask questions when I got back. It was also Mrs Lawson's birthday. At ten, George Charlesworth and I pushed Stan off and got on with the notes. Peter was on call. He said he would be in to say goodbye, but had not returned when I was ready to go. George said he would explain. 'He'll miss you. One does—miss people.'

Dolly's holiday ended tomorrow. She had only returned temporarily for the ball. Suddenly I not only felt very sorry, but a new respect for George. Even after working with him and Dolly, I had not guessed their one-sided relationship until Peter told me. Obviously, Miss Evans had not heard, and only Peter and Dolly had mentioned it to me. I wondered if unselfishness failed to make news because it was unspectacular, or so rare that nine out of ten people didn't believe it when they saw it. Then I wondered how long it would take Dolly to believe it, or if her early background was going to leave her a permanent emotional cripple. That left me feeling so dispirited when I got back to the flat that I was very glad Roxanne was out at a party. I wept over my packing as I had not wept in ages and when I let the little woman in me have her head, I never had cared for an audience.

Roxanne was free next morning and only woke about ten minutes before I left. 'Say that again, Cathy! What domestic issues?'

'God alone knows!'

She unwound a few dozen curlers. 'You are fierce! All this hard work. Very bad for the soul. A jolly jaunt is just what you need—'

'Jolly? Prof. Ulvik's four years off eighty and St Peter held those gates open for about a fortnight.'

'Joss said it was a damned close-run thing and the only two people who thought he'd make it were the old boy himself, and you. Joss says he's good value. So's Joss. And he keeps his hands to himself. I wouldn't mind an orge in Norge with him, even if his heart is in the Highlands.'

'Edinburgh is in Midlothian. The Lowlands.'

She laughed. 'Never mind, dear. With any luck you'll hit a Force Ten gale and all be revoltingly sick before the ship goes down.' My taxi had arrived. 'Any last message for your next-of-kin?'

I smiled reluctantly. 'Yes. Peter's interview for this Leeds job is now this Monday. I forgot to wish him luck. Ring him for me and don't be surprised if he sounds incoherent. Interviews and exams always reduce him to a pea-green jelly.'

The Alesunds had hired a chauffeur-driven car to take us from Asden General to the ship's berth at Newcastle. The Professor was escorted down the front steps of the hospital and into the car by the Matron, Assistant Matron, a registrar, houseman, two sisters, and a posse of nurses. Though on elbow crutches, he towered over everyone present and his white, blue-veined hands looked far too frail to lift a walking-stick, much less support him. He did allow his ward sister to lift his plastered leg into the back of the car while a nurse held his crutches. All other offers of help were dismissed with polite firmness. 'Many thanks. I manage!'

'Don't crack that plaster before you get home, Professor! See you in Bergen!'

Joss was in front. He turned round to us as we drove off waving like royalty. 'Invited them all to stay, sir?'

'Yoss, of course, of course!' The old man's face was as white as his hair and withered by illness as well as age. His very blue eyes seemed to belong to another man. They were vivid with intelligence and humour and were decades younger than the face from which they looked on the world. 'One of the few advantages of becoming a monument—and to become one it is necessary to pass three score years and ten—is that one can encourage pretty women to visit the monument in his home, without causing offence to any.' He studied me, thoughtfully. 'So. You are Miss Catherine Maitland? How do you do, Miss Catherine Maitland?'

We had already shaken hands. We did so again. 'How do you do, Professor?'

'Ah, ha!' He clapped his hands. 'I love the English! A pretty girl helps to save my life—I break my old bones—I am in hospital many weeks—but do we discuss this? No, no, no! We ask each other how we do, and neither must give the answer. Not on! That is the correct idiom, now? And, is it—on—to presume to call you Cathy? As Yoss?' He wrinkled his nose. 'That terrible English J! Not for my aged Norwegian tongue, or I would do—as the good sister frequently assured me—myself a great mischief.'

144

He slept some of the long drive. Awake, he did not talk a great deal, but when he did he was very amusing. And astute. 'So, Cathy? You are surprised at such levity from the aged Professor? I tell you something! The Norwegian is the Scandinavian Irishman. Did you ever meet the Irishman too old to enjoy a good joke in good company? Now I have made the poor child blush! Yoss, discuss the weather! In moments of embarrassment the English always discuss the weather. This I have observed many times in many years.'

I changed my mind about Arne Alesund's remark before the ship was out of the Tyne. The Professor treated newly scrubbed decks, polished floors, stairs and companionways as trivial hazards to be ignored. After Joss had saved him from slipping for the third time by taking his weight whilst I collected the dropped crutches, I said quietly, 'He needs more muscle-power than I've got.'

Joss looked at me, hard. 'If you're feeling sick, ask the stewardess for those pills she's doling out.'

We had three single cabins in a row. The Professor was in the middle. He rested after we sailed, but refused dinner in bed. 'I have eaten too many meals alone. Tonight, I give a little party.'

I caught Joss's eye and shook my head, doubtfully. He gave me an ugly look in return and when we left to freshen up told me to stop being a bloody wet blanket. 'So he's putting the pressure on himself. How in hell would he've survived what he just has, if he hadn't? He's going home, not improbably for the last time, and he wants to celebrate. Sulk as much as you like on the way back, but tonight we're going to bloody celebrate. Or are you feeling sick? You're a filthy colour.'

I reminded him I was never sea-sick and had not spent the last week on holiday. 'Or have you forgotten what the A.U. can be like?'

'No. Nor one hideous moment I spent in the damned

Unit!' He went into his cabin and closed the door. He hadn't called it 'the Unit' since Butler left it. I wished I hadn't noticed, and then, as pointlessly, that the last rush had not left me so extraordinarily tired. Dinner was a nightmarish thought as I wasn't hungry, but when it came, I enjoyed it. The Professor was in tremendous form and the food and wine were excellent. 'Now, another toast. Skål, Cathy! No, no, Yoss, not so! When you say "skål" you must look into the eyes of the one you toast whilst you finish your drink. I watch you! Better! I think now I will retire and you must join the dancing, eh?'

We did not argue then, or later, when he was settled for the night. I said, 'Joss, I'm too sleepy.'

'You look it. 'Night.'

I slept ten hours which probably accounted for my waking with such a headache. Despite dark glasses, the glare hurt my eyes. I turned my back on the sea and the Professor lowered his newspaper. He was lying in a cane deckchair against the sun-deck bulkhead behind us. 'Is the North Sea often this calm in late September, Professor?'

'Sometimes, yes. Sometimes, all month she rages and roars. The North Sea, as every sea, being as unpredictable as woman is to man.' He threw aside his rug as the ship altered speed to turn into the fjord. 'Stavanger! Good. I join you. And this afternoon—Bergen.'

We steadied him between us at the rail as we glided into the blue mirror of the fjord and the mountains curved behind us, shutting out the sea. As we neared the green arm of the harbour, a small fleet of fishing boats chugged by seawards, and countless little black and white ferries pottered around us like water beetles. 'Buses,' said the Professor. 'You go by road. We go by water.'

The tiny white wooden box houses with red, green, blue and grey roofs covering the steep slopes surrounding the harbour stopped looking like toys. We were close enough to see the colours of the curtains and in practically every

146

window, rows of potted plants blooming in contented domestic jungles.

'Good!' The old man's sigh was contented as the engines stopped. 'Now, no delay as there is little time. I'll stay in my cabin whilst you two go ashore.' He waved aside our instant objections. 'So you will see Stavanger on your return? I will tell you something! No man can foresee or promise tomorrow. Tomorrow is either a hope or a dream. Today, and only today, we live. Today, a new land is waiting for you. But life does not wait, happiness does not wait, and nor, alas, does youth, or this ship! You have only two hours. Off! Off!'

Ten minutes later Joss knocked on my door with our landing passes. He raised his eyebrows at my coat. 'Chilly?'

I had just taken my temperature and a couple of anti-cold tablets. I did not feel strong enough for the truth, or another crack about wet blankets. 'Thought I might need it ashore after this central heating. Shouldn't we look in on the Prof. to say we're off?'

'I've just told him and our stewardess.' He walked off leaving me to trail after him like an Arab wife. He did wait at the foot of the gangway. 'What do you want to do? Drift? Or make for anywhere special?'

I wanted to lie down and die. 'Drift. You?'

He had a look round. 'Same.' He smiled. 'Not another country. Another world. These are docks!'

I pushed up my dark glasses for a better look and thought of the grime and noise in the docks round Martha's. The little harbour was busy, but the quiet and the cleanliness were as soothing as they were incredible to our alien eyes. We drifted at first in a rather tense silence, and then in a kind of dream, stopping and moving on, without words.

We stopped some time to watch the water slapping like oil against the little boats tied up to the edge. Boats piled with green vegetable, potatoes, fresh fruit, baskets and baskets of crabs.

I jumped back. 'Joss, those crabs! They're walking out!'

He laughed. A long thin fisherman in a yellow jersey, jeans and red pom-pom hat waved at us. 'You wish to buy my crabs? Best crabs,' he said in English, 'only from me!'

'Not today, thanks!' We waved and moved on.

A little way on, a small boy was fishing with a bit of herring fixed to a bent pin on a piece of string. 'God,' muttered Joss, 'this takes me back. The hours I fished the dykes at home and hardly ever caught anything—which reminds me. Mother says it's a long time since you were down for a weekend. I explained you wouldn't have one for a couple of weeks but if you can make that one it'll suit her, as Dan'll be away and I'll be back on the job. Plenty of room.'

It was an ideal moment for explaining about my holiday. I did not take it. I might have done, had the previous moments not been so tranquil. I said I would write to his mother, simply must see the fishmarket and charged across the cobbles with the eagerness of the many house-wives choosing with experienced eyes the live fish from the open tanks. 'Ever seen so many fish?' I was talking to myself. Joss did not reappear until I reached a sealskin slippers stall several minutes later. 'Come and see what I've found, Cathy.'

He took me across the road to the small and glorious mosaic of colour that was the flower-market. He vanished again between the banks of bronze, orange, yellow and white chrysanthemums and I ambled past the azaleas and cyclamen to the roses. Roses red, pink, yellow, near-mauve, and all exquisitely scented. The long-stemmed yellow tea-roses reminded me of my father's pleasure when he took a First at the county show with either the identical or a very similar variety. I touched one unthinkingly as I tried to recall the name. The stout lady

148

behind the stall lifted it from the bunch. 'You wish?'

'Yes, please.' Joss's voice answered. I glanced round and he thrust a huge bunch of chrysanthemums at me. 'For Nina. Prof. says she fancies them.' He paid for the rose. 'What are these called? Didn't your father get his First with them?'

'Yes. And couldn't have been more thrilled if he'd won the pools. I can't remember the name. Isn't that awful?'

'You were only about eleven.' He retrieved the chrysanthemums and held on to the rose. 'I had a chat with my old mum about you and L.B. Both very sweet, she said.' He looked round the flowers, then offered me the rose. 'Couldn't find an olive branch. In lieu of—from me to you.' He flushed slightly. 'Dead sloppy I am this morning. All this foreign travel is disorientating for an English lad.'

I wanted to cry, gently. So I laughed. 'Thanks.'

'My pleasure! Now, for God's sake, woman, move, or we'll miss the bloody ship!'

We made it within minutes of their unhitching the gangway. Our gallop had done strange things to my legs, but I put the rose in water before I registered the fact. Later, I wrapped it in wet tissues and zipped it in my sponge-bag. I felt remarkably like a deprived Victorian maiden and not only because I hadn't with me an album in which to press it.

It was evening, not afternoon, when we sailed into the Professor's home port. The towering outlines of the seven mountains of Bergen merged gently into the slowly darkening sky. The fir forests on the lower slopes were black, not green, velvet and the snow above tree level gleamed whitely in the light from the already high three-quarter moon. The water in the fjord could have been navy blue silk and as our ship moved towards her berth, she split the water with the sound of tearing silk. There were only a few stars in the sky, but the land blazed with millions stretching upwards from the harbour to what appeared to

149

be half-way up the mountains. 'If we have one thing in Norway,' said the Professor, 'we have water. So, cheap electricity. So, we leave our lights on. Electricity is much cheaper than the new switches.'

He was again at the rail between us, but this time when the engines stopped, he did not say a word. Joss and I kept quiet. The expression on the old man's face said all that needed to be said. No aged and frail professor, but a tough old Viking, had sailed safely home.

The Alesunds, their son, the Professor's elder widowed daughter, her two teenagers, Arne's brother with his wife and sub-teen sons were all waiting. The reunion was affectionate, dignified and infinitely moving. Very little was said as we drove in four cars to the Alesunds' house. The Professor had lived with them since his wife's death some years ago.

The front door was open. The two little girls in dressing-gowns were waiting in the hall with Arne's parents. By unspoken consent, everyone stood aside to let the Professor walk alone through the front door, and then, with a tidal wave of emotion, the entire family engulfed him.

Joss handed me a clean handkerchief. 'Haven't seen you weep since you got measles on your eighth birthday.'

'Ninth,' I wailed. 'And what's wrong with my fancying a bit of slop?'

'Nothing's wrong, dearie. There, there—' he patted then gripped my hand and his manner changed. 'You're running a temp,' he said very quietly.

Nina had remembered us. 'Come in! Come in!' My face caused no comment as every woman present was now happily mopping her eyes. After one, and dynamic, drink to the Professor's return and a fresh orgy of handshaking and congratulations, we were taken to our rooms to change for the massive dinner party due directly the smaller children were in bed. 'Late for them,' said Nina, 'but a great family occasion they had to share.'

Arne put down my suitcase. 'Speaking frankly, we are a family-minded people. You join us soon, no? We will have a great celebration!'

I smiled till they closed the door then flopped on the bed. The aquavite had finished me off. Incapable of thought, I lay with my eyes closed listening to Arne explaining to Joss the finer points of the new bathroom they had installed between the guest rooms that were later to be the girls' bedrooms. Then Joss said something about remembering he needed something I had for him in my case and had knocked on my door and come in before I was off the bed. He shut the door and leant against it. 'Second time round?'

I flopped back. 'I've been hoping not all afternoon, but I'm horribly afraid so. I could kill myself for bringing it here. What am I going to do?'

He did not answer, at first. He came and sat on the side of the bed, took my pulse, felt my forehead with the back of his hand, looked down my throat, then fingered the glands in my neck. He produced a thermometer, shook it down and smiled very kindly. 'Speaking frankly, darling, I suggest your best bet is to call me Sister Florence.'

Chapter Twelve

The house had been built on a small plateau blasted out of the side of a mountain. The window of my room over-looked the roofs of tower flats and box houses similarly perched and a fjord below. Across the water were high green hills and then mountains rising one behind the other as they had from the sea, and their colour kept changing. Black, blue, sepia, purple; each time I looked a different shade, each time the same impression of continuing to eternity.

From Friday night to Tuesday morning that was my only view of Norway. By mutual consent, since the elderly and very young are particularly susceptible to 'flu and its complications and the household included both age groups, Joss was my only human contact. The very little nursing I needed, he did very well. And he never came in without a message of regret and sympathy from one of the family. On Sunday evening he delivered another from the Professor with my supper-tray. I said I was sorry to be in purdah, but even yesterday when I had felt like death, it had been a tremendous relief that the family had the intelligence to realize that this was the only way to cut down the risk.

'That doesn't so much need intelligence as imagination.

152

Much rarer, but they've got it.' He put the tray on the dressing stool he had turned into a bed-table. 'Not hungry? Don't let it bug you. What you can't eat I'll get rid of before anyone sees it when I wash up.' He sat on the foot of my bed. He was wearing a white drip-dry, scarlet cravat and black cords and looked very nice. He tanned easily and after the sea and northern air he could have been in the sun weeks. 'Nina's given me a fish-kettle as my crockery sterilizer. I now know why nurses have asbestos hands. Two days on the job, and I can pluck anything from boiling water.'

My temperature an hour ago had been normal for the first time since I took it in Stavanger. We hoped that was because I had the forty-eight-hour type, but as I was packed with aspirin and prophylactic antibiotics it was too early to tell. Joss, like every other doctor I knew of, never travelled without his private emergency supply of the latter. That saved us bothering Nina's doctor, and as I had started coughing on Friday night, very probably saved me from having bronchitis. I now had no trace of a cough and was feeling sufficiently better to be conscious I looked a wreck and thoroughly peevish. 'Your halo, Joss, is blinding me.'

He laughed. 'Thank God, yours has slipped! Your unnerving docility has had me wondering if I should ring Canada. Did I tell you Arne's contacted the shipping company? Sorry, thought I had—' he added before I could raise an objection. 'Obviously, you can't travel tomorrow—'

'Joss, if it's the forty-eight hour—can't I?'

'Over my dead body, dearie,' he said pleasantly, 'and Arne's, and Nina's, and the Prof.'s—may I go on?' I nodded, glumly. 'The company have been very decent. If you're clear, they can fix us up on Wednesday, if not on the next ship back, which'll be Saturday. The Alesunds are hoping that's what it'll be—my God!'

'Wednesday you're due in Edinburgh?'

153

'No. I've written to Naomi and chums. But I haven't written to Miss Evans. Could be time, but to be safe I had better cable. What time are you due on on Wednesday?'

'I'm not.' I fiddled with my salmon mousse and explained. There was a short silence. Then, 'That's handy.'

I looked up and he looked out of the window. 'Miss Evans didn't tell me what domestic reasons.'

'She wouldn't, as they're strictly personal. Not that I feel the cloak and dagger are necessary, but I'm not Naomi.' He faced me, slowly. 'Handy, but the hell of a waste of a holiday.'

'Not exactly fun for you, home-nursing in foreign parts. Dead bore.'

'That what you think?' He winced extravagantly. 'There goes my ego! I've been fancying myself with my lamp!'

'Joss, to be fair—'

'For God's sake, don't now tell me I've got a vocation, or I'll know you're having a relapse. Oak or elm? As you were—wrong country—pine? And do you positively insist on brass handles?'

I smiled weakly. 'You are a fool! No. You do lay a real cool hand on a fevered brow.'

'Watch it, or you'll get my cool hands round your fevered throat.' He stood up, smiling. 'We ministering angels have our feelings. I shall now go and soothe mine by having the remains of my ego hammered by the Prof.'

' 'More chess? But you're very good.'

He shook his head. 'Not in his league. Whatever ails his leg, his brain's first-rate.'

'Is his leg playing up?'

'No more than one would expect seeing what he does with it. He's scaring the daylights out of us all with the chances he takes, but as he says, plenty of time to rest when he's dead.' He nodded at my tray. 'You eat all that up and you'll grow into a big strong girl and be able to go home on Wednesday.'

154

I did a Dolly with my eyelashes. 'Yes, Sister Florence.'

'Wait.' he said, 'wait until you see me in my purple satin. That'll really send you.' He blew me a kiss and went off smiling. I went right off my food, but forced it down. He was being so damned kind, I had to co-operate. For the same reason, when he tentatively suggested next day ringing his mother and my going straight to the vicarage to convalesce until the weekend when he presumed I would want to be back in London, I agreed. I would have done so had he suggested I convalesced on the next moon-shot. He promptly took my temperature. 'I thought so. Subnormal. Depression setting in nicely. Whose throat do you want to cut first? Yours or mine?'

My temperature stayed down and none of the family showed any signs of catching my 'flu, or went down with it later. At the farewell dinner-party on Tuesday night, Arne's brother Olaf suggested I had picked up an indigenous variety from some fellow-traveller and that could account for them all having some immunity. Olaf, a lawyer, was the elder and better-looking brother, though neither could be described as anything but plain. They were both large men with powerful shoulders, egg-shaped heads with scrubbing-brush hair-cuts and pale blue eyes that in repose had the same strange innocence I had first noticed in Nina's, but seemed even stranger in obviously successful professional men in their mid-thirties. I had never seen that innocence in the face of any adult Englishman of any age or background.

Joss said, 'This is quite possible, Cathy, and why it hit you so hard, though it's obviously a milder, shorter variety.'

'Then why didn't you get it?'

'I just don't get 'flu now.'

There was a universal groan. 'Joss,' I exclaimed, 'how can you so smugly ask for trouble?'

'I wasn't being smug. Just stating a fact.' He looked

155

round the candle-lit table. Being a gala occasion, the cheap electricity was turned off. 'English hospitals have some kind of 'flu epidemic every year. Don't ask me how I've missed out, year after year. I just have.'

Nina said, 'I know why! There is an English poet—what is it—a pure heart?'

'His strength,' observed the Professor drily, 'is as the strength of ten because his heart is pure. Alfred Lord Tennyson.'

Joss raised his glass. 'Skål, Nina.'

The Professor's blue eyes had seen too much for innocence. He glanced from me to Joss. 'I have known learned psychiatrists who would say you owed your good health not to any immunity from any virus, but from an immunity to the desire to escape into illness. Is that so? Ah, no!' He answered himself. 'That is a foolish question since such desires are too deep in the sub-conscious to be—to be—fished up, at will. Or even for us to be aware of their presence. The layers of the sub-conscious go deeper than the depth of the Atlantic and are as crowded with blind, unknown shapes as are the deep waters. But, I tell you something! Something less serious but of great interest. Have you looked upon an octopus, eh?'

'Octopus?' Joss echoed as the entire family bellowed with laughter.

The Professor said they could laugh, but only because the octopus had not climbed out of the sea before man. 'I tell you! Such is the intelligence of that marine creature —nothing in the sea can compare. Such grace, such delicacy, has the suckered arms of that mollusc—such wisdom in that head—' he turned to me. 'You have not seen our Aquarium. Next time, I take you. Next time, we will have a great party. In Bergen we know how to give great parties, no?'

'Speaking frankly,' said Arne, 'yes! Bring Cathy back soon, Joss!'

'Very soon,' added Nina.

'You understand, Yoss? We will not wait too long for this next party. No waiting.' The Professor raised his glass. 'Now we drink a little toast to our English guests.' He hauled himself up on the arms of his high-backed chair and balanced on his good leg and one hand on the table. Joss and I alone remained seated and staring at our plates. 'To Cathy and Yoss, but for whom three of us would not be here tonight. Skål.'

'Skål,' chorused the family.

We thanked them and rose with our own glasses.

'One minute, Yoss.' The old man looked at us with an odd little smile. 'One more, then you may make a pretty speech, eh? First, I ask you two something. At Christmas, you've seen the tree from Norway in London?'

'Every year.'

'You know why it is there?'

We both flushed. Joss said, 'Well—er—nice gesture after the war.'

'A nice gesture?' The Professor nodded to himself. 'Very English. So, I tell you something, my young, very English, friends.' He looked slowly at the faces of his family. 'It is my belief and one I share with all here old enough to remember, that we are in this room tonight, because of your country.' He paused as the elders nodded, then went on in an unemotional tone that heightened the emotional moment. 'We saw our world collapse. We heard the world say England must collapse and our hearts were sick with the despair men only know when hope is dying. But England did not collapse. And we could hope again. Without hope, man is finished. With hope, the impossible is possible. Your country—do not forget—your country alone—gave back hope to Europe and maybe, the world. So, we send you a tree.' He lifted his glass. 'The toast is England.'

157

Leaning on the rail as the ship inched from the land next morning, Joss said, 'Follow that, he said.'

'You did all right.' I borrowed a handkerchief to wave back at the farewell party on the quay. The turn-out was even larger than on our arrival, as it now included the elder Alesunds and two little girls. Arne's mother had kissed us both. 'Such a heavy boy for you to carry. Such a heavy boy! Not goodbye. Until next time!'

Every adult repeated those last five words. The children echoed them parrot-wise, shouting them over and over through the fine rain as they waved wild, macaroni arms. The Professor was doing his stork act on his good leg and had his second crutch tucked under his arm like a walking stick to free his hand waving a red-spotted handkerchief. Joss said we had better get behind the sun-lounge glass before the old man finally broke his back slipping, or I got pneumonia. 'Feeling like chewed string? Sit down and I'll get us a drink. Or are you too wet?' He seemed about to touch my coat then changed his mind and put his hand in his pocket.

'Hasn't gone through.'

I sat on the arm of a chair, watching the tugs pulling and pushing our ship right across the harbour to turn us round. The rain turned much heavier, the fjord was gunmetal, and the greyness matched my mood. And Joss's. When he came back with our drinks, he stood fairly near, but we did not talk.

The huge warehouses on the waterside shrank to match-boxes; the yellow, the blue, the green, the tan, the white box houses changed back into toys; the seven mountains of Bergen receded behind the curtain of water and the ship's screws began to throb. The dark mountains round the entrance to the fjord were ominously close and their crests were hidden in the low sky. Just there, the fjord turned a dramatic emerald green, and the alteration of the ship's motion was as dramatic when we moved into the cold grey and impatient sea.

158

I steadied myself against the gentle roll as I got off the chair. 'Would you mind if I go and get things organized in my cabin?'

Joss shot me a rather peculiar look but only said that was a good idea and he'd do the same.

We were returning by another ship, but being from the same company our single berth upper deck cabins were almost identical with those on the outward voyage, though now side by side. This had vastly amused our hosts. 'Boy and girl next door again, eh?' I had laughed dutifully, but felt if I heard that corny joke again I would probably scream. When we reached our doors, Joss unlocked mine for me, handed me back the key and unlocked his own. 'I'll give you a shout for second lunch,' he said as the occupant of the third in the trio came into the narrow corridor.

She was a solid lady in sensible tweeds with short iron-grey hair battened down with a black velvet bandeau. 'Fellow Brits homeward bound? Miss Bilson!' Her handshake hurt. 'Just down from the Arctic Circle. Been up there? You should! Wonderful skies, wonderful sunsets. D.V., I'll go back! Always return when possible. First—look-see; second—get the feel. Used to tell my girls—taught forty years for my sins—you can't get the feel of a poem, picture, or place at first sight. Get the taste second time and never gulp. No taste when you gulp.' Her small eyes appraised us and my ungloved hands with interest rather than curiosity. 'Only done this crossing once? Mind some advice from an old salt? They say the sea may be choppy, which means roughly a Force 7 to 8 gale. Take a couple of anti-seasick tablets before we leave Stavanger and you'll enjoy your dinner tonight—particularly you, young woman! Bit green round the gills, already—but forgive me! First sitting! I must rendezvous with the cold table!' She bounded off.

I leant against my doorway. 'Never have I felt so inadequate.'

159

Joss smiled politely and suggested I put my feet up until lunch. After lunch he suggested I had an afternoon snooze. Whilst the ship was in Stavanger we drank coffee in the lounge and read good books. He provided me with a social history of England and himself with one on Scotland. 'I thought you only read history before and during exams, Joss?'

'No.' He didn't look up. 'To each his own form of escapism.'

I watched covertly his intent, unguarded face. With his present tan he could be a southern Italian until he opened his mouth. Not really good-looking, but the type of looks that turned every female head in the dining-room and this lounge. I thought of a remark some woman made to Byron. 'I shall long remember the gentleness of your manner and the wild originality of your countenance.' I knew what she meant.

He glanced up. I looked quickly at my book until my ears stopped drumming. We continued reading till the ship sailed. Watching the whole process while we were at supper, Joss switched back to the fraternal heartiness he had brought to a fine art over the weekend. As we knew each other too well, I knew we were equally relieved when I went to bed early.

One of the things that weekend underlined for me was the effect of early childhood on adult character. Being the eldest child in our two families 'looking after the girls' had been bred into Joss before he lost his milk teeth. Also, consideration. As children we had known—as children invariably do—that while his parents loved him, his father had preferred Ruth, and his mother Danny. They were a singularly devoted couple and possibly when Joss had been born had unconsciously resented his intrusion. My father frequently said the odd child out in any family generally ended up the pick of the bunch if only because he or she early learnt the necessities of adaptability and unselfishness. 'Providing the child's character is strong enough to shrug off the inevitable chip.' Having been the apple of his eye and Paul of my mother's, in his lifetime I had not properly understood that. I had begun to do so in Canada, and, as I only clearly saw now, that was mainly why I had returned to England. Finding oneself for the first time in one's life as an outsider in one's own family was a disturbing experience. In my case, so disturbing that I had not dared face it until I got right away. As my bunk pitched and rolled, not unpleasantly as I had taken Miss Bilson's advice, I wondered uneasily how far I would have to get away from Joss, before I could view him as dispassionately. Then I wondered about Naomi's problem and Joss's burying himself in Scottish history. If the past was any guide to the present, all three of us had our problems, right now.

England had appeared on the horizon when Miss Bilson bounded into the lounge next morning. I was ready to go ashore and obediently waiting with my dressing-case and handbag, while Joss dealt with our other luggage and tips. 'How's the invalid this morning? Miserable complaint, *la grippe*! Rather break a leg. Broke one last year on Kilimanjaro—second time up, fortunately. Sleep well? Yes, indeed, thanks! Sleep like a top rocked in the cradle of the deep—sleep like a top, anywhere, D.G.! Had a very pleasant bridge game with your young man last night— plays a good hand—said he didn't care for dancing— still, thought it very decent of him to make up a fourth with three old fogies—and here he is and the good old U.K.!' She wrecked my knuckles for the day. '*Bon voyage*, ashore! No, thank you, Mr Desmond, I'll manage my own bags—always travel light. Toodle pip, if I don't see you on the train!'

Joss surprised me by saying we should have a self-drive hired car waiting and offering her a lift.

'How kind! How very kind! But one of my Old Girls

is meeting me in London and then I'm Devonshire-bound. Enjoy your drive, south-east. What time do you expect to be home?'

'With luck, six to seven.'

I waited till we were alone. 'Why didn't you tell me the Alesunds had fixed this up?'

'Assumed you knew. Sorry. Ready?'

'Hang on a moment.' I sat down. 'There'll be the usual queue at customs and immigration and there's something I want to sort out.' I looked up as he remained standing and watching me with his eyelids lowered and eyebrows up. 'Joss, I haven't asked your immediate plans as, well, none of my business, but, obviously, between us, the Alesunds and I've messed them up, good. When does your holiday end?'

'Next Friday. I can still have a clear week in Scotland.'

'But we're two-thirds of the way up.'

'And my car is in Asden. This set-up suits me fine. The Newcastle firm supplying today's car have a reciprocal arrangement with the garage where I've left mine. We'll change cars at Asden, I'll drop you off at home and after a meal and a bath get back to London as I've a heavy date there tonight, but not until tennish so I should make it easily. Tomorrow I'll drive north.'

It was absurd to feel so deflated. 'Good thing you like driving.'

'Isn't it?' He picked up my dressing case. 'Come on.'

After he had signed for and we were in the waiting car, I said there was something else I had to say and thanked him for looking after me like a Dutch Uncle.

He smiled quietly. 'Thanks, darling. Nice to be appreciated. Too bad these docks don't run to a flower market or you could buy me a rose—which reminds me! On the 'phone mother said if you don't feel up to London on Saturday, ask Peter down as she and the old man'll be delighted to meet him. He is off, isn't he?'

'Yes.' I glanced at my dressing-case in the back. The rose was still in my sponge-bag. 'He only had Monday as an extra for this interview.'

'What interview?'

I explained as he drove off. He thought it a splendid idea. 'Peter'll enjoy being a G.P. and he should do a good job, though as your father would say, he won't get much of a chance till he gets himself a wife. Oh—Gawd!' He sighed. 'This traffic is bloody awful and I don't know my Newcastle. Mind if the lad concentrates till we're clear?'

'Of course not. Sorry I forgot what hell driving is when one doesn't know the roads.'

He slowed to glance at me. 'Yep. Death would be a happy release. Sooner I get you home to dear old mum, the better. This unnerving docility is wrecking my vibrations. Much more, and I'll have to start taking my own temperature.'

'Sorry—or is that the wrong thing to say?'

He smiled in answer. We did not talk again till we stopped for an early lunch in York.

He rang his home after our early tea in Cambridge. His mother had a W.I. and his father an Organ Fund meeting that evening but both hoped to be home by eight. We made such good time that we could only have missed their departure by a few minutes. The ground-floor hall light had been left on when he drew up in the vicarage drive. Momentarily, after switching off, he rested both arms on the wheel and his shoulders sagged. 'What was that you said about my liking driving?'

'Shoulders seized-up?'

'Uh-huh. They'll unseize in a bath. Let's get in.' He heaved himself out and unloaded the luggage from the boot of his own and smaller car. 'Stiff?'

'Bit.' I felt more limp than my first day out of bed. I knew as surely as I knew my own name, this was the end of the road. We had been alone since noon yesterday. He had not even touched my hand, accidentally. Why should he? What normal man wanted to touch his sister's hand?

He unlocked the front door. 'Supper'll be eight-thirtyish. Mother said don't wait up if you want to go straight to bed and anyway there'll be tea and sandwiches waiting in the school-room.'

I trailed in behind him. 'Your mother's a remarkable woman. She thinks of everything.'

'She does.' He sorted the post on the hall table. 'One for you.'

'Me?' I took the envelope curiously. 'Peter! How does he know I'm here?'

He shoved his post unread in his pocket. 'Naomi said she'd be writing to Stan. He'll have told him.'

'How did she know? Didn't you say you wrote her on Saturday? This wasn't fixed till Monday.'

'No, dearie. But there is such a thing as the international telephone service.' He picked up my bags. 'Your usual room.' He went on up with them.

I followed very slowly. There was nothing to hurry for now.

Chapter Thirteen

He waited in the school-room till the electric kettle boiled, made tea, called to me to help myself and went on to his room. I heard the bath running as I poured my cup. I took it and Peter's unopened letter to one of the aged cane armchairs on either side of the heavily guarded electric convector in the hearth.

That room evoked such an attack of nostalgia that for some minutes I just sat, stared, and rode with the punch. The solid table at which, for years, Ruth and I had done our homework was covered with the old red baize cloth with a bobble fringe that went back to the years when this had been a communal nursery. The lower shelves of the white-painted bookcases were still jammed with Noddy, Big Ears, Mary Mouse; higher up the battered sagas of the March girls and Katy were crowded between William, Jennings, Jim Hawkins, rows of Percy F. Westerman, Black Beauty and the smug Swiss Robinsons. Jane Austen, Charlotte Brontë, Mrs Gaskell and Charles Dickens shared the top shelves with science fiction, Dorothy L. Sayers, Agatha Christie and Ellery Queen. And the tatty grey carpet shared with the blue hearth-rug the same fading ink stains. The room as always smelt faintly of lead, Plasticine, carbolic soap, and for some reason we had never been able to trace, burnt toast.

I dragged myself back to the present, opened Peter's letter without enthusiasm, but for once was relieved and not appalled by its length. Peter either communicated on paper with three words on a postcard, or not less than six closely written case-history sheets. He never used normal writing-paper, even for airmail.

The first two sheets concerned his interview. I read slowly, as it gave me something else to think about. Though convinced he had made a hideous impression, he thought it would have been much worse had Roxanne not decided to visit her father and hold his, Peter's, hand. She had been very sweet, he wrote, and took him to tea with her father, but he wished I had warned him Mr Alder looked exactly like a middle-aged Hamlet. He wished I hadn't got 'flu, as he wanted to talk to me about Roxanne. Mr Alder had suggested they both spend this coming weekend with him in Leeds. Roxanne seemed to think it a good idea. Peter thought it a good idea. Did I? And if so could I ring him before Saturday? Stan said I would be at the Desmonds. 'Stan—' but the sheets were in the wrong order. I searched smiling hugely for the correct follow-on. '—had a letter from our Naomi yesterday and is being hellish smug whilst the A.U. reels as Joss had tipped him off. Expect you know all from him now, but in case you don't, get this!'

I had to read the next item three times before it got thought it would have been much worse had Roxanne

Two weeks ago in Malta, Naomi Butler had married quietly a Benedict's man called Ian MacDonald to whom she had previously been twice engaged. 'Seems after the last great out-falling, she shook the dust of Benedict's from her apron and crossed the river, and didn't see him again till he visited her in Florence. (And why weren't we told? Someone has blundered—though Stan says he reckons folk never see what they don't want to see.) Anyway, chap then followed her to Malta. Stan says sun either opened her eyes or blinded her, but she sounds dead chuffed and her new in-laws likewise. She said she'd waited to write until after she had met them as they weren't at or warned about the wedding and she felt it would be incorrect to make it public before meeting them. I said what was wrong with a joyful cable? Stan says nothing unless you have a fixation for doing the correct thing the correct way and that's the way that wins gold medals. I still think she slipped up when she opted for our A.U. to give herself time to think. Who has time to think in any A.U.—or wants it? Get this next—'

I could not, for the moment. I put down the letter, drank some tea, and breathed very, very carefully. Joss knew and had known some time. Joss was driving to London tonight, Scotland tomorrow. The question was—since her name wasn't Naomi, what was it? Fiona? Catriona? How the hell could I know? I just knew Joss and young men in general. When one was determined, come what may to get from A to B, commonest things being the most common, the girl he most wanted was at B. I picked up the last page.

'—this morning George, Dolly and I had to go out in a Crash Call ambulance. First time in months and I don't fancy a repeat. Spot on the clearway just beyond the flyover. When we arrived, all we could see at first was twisted tin flung all round the road and a bloody great red pool in the middle. George stooped to pick up what we thought was some poor sod's false teeth. Cath, they were not false. We found the chap who owned them in five separate pieces. . . .'

'God, no!' I dropped the sheet and buried my face in my hands as my stomach contracted.

'What the devil has that fool written to do this to you?' Joss's urgent voice was very close. I lowered my hands to find him bending over me.

'Read this.' The page shook as I held it out. 'That last paragraph.'

He backed as if offered a ticking bomb. 'Don't be so bloody silly! I'm not reading another man's letter to his girl!'

'Don't *you* be bloody silly!' Even my voice was shaking. 'Would I be handing it to you if it were—I was—oh hell —you know what I mean! Read it!'

His X-ray glance couldn't have been improved by Miss Mackenzie, but he did as I said. His face twisted. 'Christ!' he muttered. 'The impact must've been around one hundred and forty.'

'Joss, please—skip it. I know it's my job—I'll go back to it—but just now I haven't the guts to take it. Do something for me?' He gave me another X-ray as he nodded. 'See if there's anything more then will I ring him about Leeds and love, as I can't face the rest. Is that all?'

Again, he hesitated, then obliged. 'Apart from saying Roxanne'll ring you over the weekend.' He folded the sheet. 'She off on another telly commercial in foreign parts? And want this back?'

'No, thanks.' I pushed the other sheets into the envelope and handed it to him. 'Shove it in there and then put it—oh—the back of that toy cupboard'll do. The closed one. I'll get around to shifting it some time, but I don't want to think about it now.'

He said oddly, 'Yes. You always used to sling things you wanted to forget in here.' He closed the cupboard doors. 'How did Leeds go?'

'I think, very hopeful.' With the letter hidden I was glad of a cheering subject. After telling him Peter's personal news, I smiled slightly. 'With any luck, this is my swan-song as his favourite teddy bear. Incidentally, you were right. Stan told him I'd be here and has heard from Naomi. In—some detail.'

'You mean she's told him she's finally had the sense to

marry Ian MacDonald. If the Archangel Gabriel isn't a Scot he should be, seeing that chap's patience. God knows I wouldn't have put up with what he has, though there's a lot I like about Naomi.' He refilled my cup and poured himself one. 'I'm glad she's written to Stan. He's such a nice chap even she likes him—and she never has taken kindly to the human race—or not until she knows said race well. That takes her a good three years. Doesn't mix easily. Some don't.'

He had sounded as if talking in one language and thinking in another, but being preoccupied, it took me a little time to notice both that and his changed appearance. He had on his best dark suit, clean white shirt, Benedict's tie and had had a shave. He looked incongruously smooth in this setting, disturbingly attractive, and, I realized belatedly, very angry.

That tie always had worried me. I had to test the untested ice. 'Your date tonight at Benedict's?'

'Yep.' He glanced at the closed toy cupboard. 'You're all for Roxanne taking Peter off your back?'

'I'll say! I'm very fond of old Pete, and he's one of my best friends, but to be thoroughly corny, there comes a time when the best of friends must part and I think that time has come if only as life in the A.U. provides me with enough problems. Once I used to enjoy collecting all my friends. Not any more. Haven't the energy. Maybe I'm getting old.'

'Everyone feels that way after 'flu.'

'This isn't post-'flu. This has been coming on for some time, but I didn't know how to break the habit without hurting his feelings. That I didn't and wouldn't want to do.'

'A touchingly faithful teddy bear.'

I stiffened. 'Why so superior? Isn't this—isn't this very much the set-up between you and Naomi?'

'Oh, no. Oh, no.' He walked to the bookshelves and

stood briefly with his back to me. 'As a teddy bear, sweetie—' he faced me slowly '—I'm not in your league. Far too immature. That's my trouble.'

I stood up. 'What do you mean—in my league?'

He put his hands in his pockets and looked me over as that first morning in the A.U. 'In my infantile league,' he drawled, 'the only teddy bears that get taken to bed have brown mock fur all over them and growl when you punch their stomachs.'

I blushed more with amusement than anything else. 'You don't seriously think—'

'Serious thought on holiday, darling, is something I avoid like the plague!' He looked at the table cover. 'Strange to remember I once had to stop you from chewing off those bobbles. And how you'd then beat it under the table and glare at me accusingly as a puppy denied the privilege of eating the new rug.' He looked back at me. 'But those days are long gone. You do as you like, since that's what you like to do—and I do likewise. And that, as of now, is to get moving and see my old boss at Benedict's tonight as he's tentatively offered me a job when I finish with Hoadley and I want to clinch the deal before I join up with the cohorts of MacDonalds I've promised to look up across the Border. Once my holiday ends, the year and my contract'll have ended before I next draw breath—and that can't be too bloody soon for me! I won't hang on for the parents. I'll stop by at the village hall and explain to mother. Why don't you go to bed? You look terrible.' He smiled sardonically. 'Recently, I wouldn't have said our mutual roots had many advantages, but at least it means I know I don't now have to offer you a shoulder. Poor old Peter. I'm almost sorry for him. I hope he gets a better deal from Roxanne.'

'Hold on, Joss!' I spoke between my teeth and got between him and the door. 'I don't want to wreck your future, but there are some things up with which I'm not

170

prepared to put! So who told you I'd been to bed with Peter?'

'For God's sake, don't be tedious, darling! I'm not digging dirt in this suit.'

'Then let me tell you something!' I told him the truth. 'Of course, if you've been fool enough to believe the grapevine, you won't believe me.'

His eyebrows rose languidly. 'Maybe that would impress me, had I only been put in the picture in strict confidence by no more than ten of your old chums the night before you turned up in the A.U. I'll admit after that I lost count as well as interest. But—er—as you may remember—more than once you kindly provided me with the type of evidence that does tend to lend an air of verisimilitude to an otherwise bald and unconvincing narrative. So stop pretending you're an outraged Victorian maiden since we both know only one of those epithets is applicable.'

I leant against the door. 'Are you talking about the night you brought Roxanne home from some ghastly party?'

'That could be called the highlight, though it wasn't the first or last time I've seen you in Peter's arms.' His colour had risen, too. 'The first Monday morning's reunion was touching beyond belief.'

'Don't be so moronic, Joss—he was just pleased to see me! As for that night—just bloody listen!' Again I told him the truth and this time threw in my comments to Roxanne on that occasion. 'This teddy bear doesn't much mind being cuddled by her friends,' I added, 'but she minds very much being called a liar to her face.'

He walked in silence to the far side of the table and folded his arms. His colour had so drained even his lips were white. 'Obviously I had my lines crossed. I'm sorry. I apologize.'

My anger evaporated. I had not seen him so white since

171

the day my brother smashed his new watch and my mother—unfairly, since Paul started the fight—made Joss, the bigger and older boy, apologize first. The next time Paul started a fight, my father had been watching and had had to break it up. Back in our house, when mother complained of Joss's savage temper, my father reminded her all boys were little savages under the skin, but he had never known Joss hit first. *'Cet animal est très méchant. Quand on l'attaque il se défend.'*

'Joss. Did you mind?'

'Mind?' He winced visibly. 'Cathy, have you an amnesial blank over Ruth's wedding day? Or—' he jerked his head at the toy cupboard '—have you just shoved it out of sight?'

'No, but—'

'So you remember what I said to you?' His tone was much calmer than my altered heart rhythm. 'Just didn't believe it?'

'Joss, I—'

'Yes, or no?'

'Well—yes—at first. Not after.'

'Why not? Come on! Naomi?'

'Yes, but not just her.' I needed a long breath. 'You weren't exactly forthcoming that first morning in the A.U.'

'Did you expect me to be? Having heard *ad nauseam* Cathy Maitland was returning from Canada to Peter Anthony's waiting arms, I walk in and—surprise, surprise —clinch just breaking up. What was I supposed to do? Tap him on the shoulder and say, mate, you don't know what you missed on Saturday night? As I didn't—you just wrote me off?'

'No—oh, hell, Joss! I thought—well—after the wedding, the soft lights, sweet music—you know what I mean!'

'Do I?' He flushed, darkly. 'You're damned right, I do! As the Prof. would say, Cathy, I will tell you something! I never thought my ego could take more of a bashing

172

than you gave it that afternoon here before that smash, but I was so wrong!'

'Listen, please, listen! I know that wasn't fair—'

'On the something contrary, since you thought I was having it on with one woman and making passionate passes at another, your reaction was fair bloody comment! Twenty-four years!' He slapped the table with one hand. 'You've had twenty-four years to add me up and that's what you figure? Thanks very much!'

'Joss, cool it! You don't have to be hurt—'

'Don't have to be? God Almighty!' Suddenly, the lid came off. 'You stupid, insensitive little bitch, what do you think I'm made of? Expect me to enjoy being thought not merely a liar, but a lecherous bastard so short on small-talk and self-preservation that I tell all my dates I bloody love 'em and kiss 'em as I've kissed you, as a variation on chatting 'em up about the weather? And wouldn't let the fact that the woman I'm supposed to be hitched to is some place else or ill, stop me? Right little sex-maniac, am I?' He slammed the table with both hands. 'Am I? Then it's bloody lucky for you I've been off-colour this last weekend and specifically these last twenty-four hours. Right next door and all I had to do was walk in and there you'd be in another of those prim little nighties you fancy —which, incidentally, are a damn sight more seductive than anything you can see through. And did I mind having to keep my hands off? For your information, Cathy, I minded like bloody hell! As I minded having to watch you and Peter in and out of the A.U.! And having to walk out on you that night after the wedding. Have you forgotten your set-up then?' He only gave me time to shake my head. 'So you've remembered you were punch-drunk from the flight, homecoming, and the champagne. Did you realize your resistance was so low you could probably have been had for the taking? God only knows why you think I didn't. By your reckoning, no

173

time'd suit me better than the time when circumstances have already obligingly lowered the girl's defences—'

'This isn't true—'

'Stuff that hypocritical docility! It was tough enough to take when I thought you were using it as a civilized way of holding me off, for Peter's sake! It's a damned effective defence, as only a sadist fancies swiping that other cheek! I never thought I was a sadist, but right now, I wouldn't bet on it! Did I mind?' He caught his breath. 'Yes! So bloody much that though you've had 'flu and I'm still fool enough to love you—nothing—nothing would give me greater pleasure than to clout you now into the middle of next week! Take my advice and stay that side of the table till I've cooled off!'

I was flattened against the door by shock and joy. I had to lick my lips to speak. 'Is it all right if I get something from my room?'

'Better still, stay there! You'll be safe! As I've told you, we sex-maniacs can go off-colour!'

I didn't risk smiling. Not yet. I opened the door, then spun round. 'You won't vanish in your car?'

'I'm not that much of a fool. If I got behind a wheel at this moment I'd be in five pieces before I was a mile out of the village.' He saw my grimace. 'I warned you, Cathy.'

'Yes.' I met his angry, hurt, and infinitely vulnerable, eyes. 'Back in a moment.' I rushed into my room, flung open my dressing-case, and then went very slowly back to the schoolroom with my sponge-bag. He had not moved. I stood at the other end of the table. 'By—er—a strange coincidence I just happen to have an olive branch in here.' I flicked the sponge-bag to him. 'As I love it quite disproportionately, I'd rather you didn't shove it down with my back teeth, but won't hold it against you if you do. But if you laugh,' I added quietly, 'I shall probably kill you with my bare hands.'

For a second time I could have offered him a ticking

bomb. Then he picked up and unzipped the bag and emptied the contents into the palm of his left hand. He stared at the dead rose and soggy brown tissues for about thirty seconds. At last, he looked over to me with an expression that held more than a hint of a resemblance to the Professor's as we sailed into Bergen. 'Have you got an album in which to press this, Cathy?' he asked unsteadily.

'No.'

'Can I give you one?'

'Yes, please.'

His face tensed, but not with anger. 'What kind do you want?'

'Huge and white with gilt edges—' my voice was uneven '—and—and a red velvet heart and lots of lovely slushy flowers on the cover.'

The tension vanished. 'It'll bore the kids—but the grandchildren'll love it.'

'That's what I thought.'

'Did you? When?'

'Well, actually, it's been in one of those cupboards since Ruth's wedding.' I smiled shyly. 'I—sort of took it out for a better look while you were pounding me to a jelly.'

'Pounding didn't worry you?'

'Shook me, but I knew you wouldn't clout me. You've threatened to clout Ruth and me, long as I can remember, but you never would and we knew it. That's why I only beat it under this table when you wouldn't let me eat the bobbles. Had you been Paul or Danny, I'd have beat it fast for one of the parents. That's why—' I spread my hands '—this weekend I thought—just old Joss doing his usual big-hearted stuff. And not knowing how it was with you and Naomi—hell—she was your type and—and only last week she got the weight of the cake right!'

'She did.' His eyes smiled wonderfully. 'Made a nice extra wedding present. She'd brought Ian down to meet the parents for the afternoon.'

'You didn't put that on your postcard!'

'It didn't seem a good idea, quite apart from the fact that she didn't want it publicized, as I suspected the Alesunds and the Prof. were determined to throw us together. To each his own defence mechanism.' He swung himself over the table as he used to as a boy and landed beside me. He did not touch me. 'Why didn't you tell me you were feeling ill at Stavanger? And on holiday? Not to lumber me?'

'Yes.' I touched his tie. 'Do you really have to leave tonight?'

'No.' He held my hand against his thudding chest. 'I can see the man any time this next week. The job he's offering is good and has a flat, rather like Stan's, thrown in. Can we talk about it, later?'

'I'd like that.'

We smiled the same smiles. He said, 'I don't have to be in Scotland. Didn't have to be in Malta. It was just somewhere to go when they shoved this holiday at me to get the books straight—out of range.'

'Of me—and Peter?'

'Yep.' He patted my flattened hand. 'You can feel what you do to me. And you, my darling, have done it since Ruth's wedding. Absurd state of affairs. Touch you and my rate goes up around one hundred and sixty, stat. Do you wonder working with you in the A.U. nearly turned me into an old man? As for this weekend—' he drew me into his arms and buried his face in my hair. 'I gathered around the house that Olaf and wife had offered to fetch the Prof. by sea, but our trio weren't having any.' He tightened his arms. 'Nor were we.'

I kissed his chin. 'The Prof. would say, very English.'

'Speaking frankly, darling, no wonder the world thinks us mad.' He raised his head to look into my face. 'Know something, Cathy? I adore you.'

'Know something, Joss? I do, you.'

176

He kissed me then as if it were years, not months, since Ruth's wedding and we had to make up for all the missing years. And then we heard his mother calling from the hall. 'Children! I'm back! Where are you?'

He gave a kind of stifled yelp that was a mixture of happiness, laughter and impatience and suddenly lifted me high in his arms. 'Up here aboard the lugger!' he yelled back.

Chapter Fourteen

The last Thursday of the year was our last working day in Martha's. We fixed to stay that night in town as the Lawsons were giving us a farewell party and we would drive down to the vicarage on Friday morning. Joss was spending Friday night with Ruth's in-laws as our wedding was on Saturday. I was marrying from the vicarage and the Vicar's brother was giving me away as he had Ruth.

The Alesunds were flying over. Professor Ulvik bombarded us with cables. 'Did I not say we would have a great celebration?'

Mrs Frayling wrote: 'How very kind of you to invite us. Yes, indeed, we remember you both. . . .'

Miss Evans said, 'Oh, dear! Oh, dear! But—how delightful!'

Being not only Thursday, but the day before New Year's Eve, we had one of the quietest as well as coldest afternoons of the winter in the A.U. The party was due to start at seven; Stan, Peter, Dave Palmer and I were off at six. Joss finished in the Orthopaedic Unit at five-forty-five. Apart from Naomi, her husband and Roxanne, all the other guests were from Martha's. 'Going to bankrupt me,' said Stan, 'so the next happy couple from the A.U. gets seen off on canteen coffee.'

George, Dolly, Henty, now an official staff nurse, Hamish Geddes and an R.A. on loan from the General Theatres were staying on to run the department with the student nurses and medics. Our two newish staff nurses were off that day to be back to support Dolly over what, in all probability, would be one of the heaviest weekends of the year. Miss Evans had firmly dismissed my tentative offer to alter the date. 'Miss Mackenzie is as satisfied as I am that Miss Jones will manage—and Miss Mackenzie is on for the weekend.'

Everyone, including the S.S.O., had co-operated over the Lawsons' party. Peter's replacement joined us at five. By half-past, we were empty.

Stan surveyed the staff-packed Receiving Room. 'Anyone for hockey? We can play it seven-a-side.' He smiled at me. 'You'll not know yourself with real work to do when you get to your new medical ward across the river, Sister.'

'Ever-so-dear sir, spare us the reminder of such treachery! A betrayal, no less!' Dave swept imaginary tears from his eyes. 'To think we took the man to our bosom—cherished him—nay—revered him—and what does he do? Swipes our Sister!' He waved at the wall clock. 'Twenty minutes from now and lost, but lost to us for ever—oh, woe!' The red light was flashing. 'Turn that off! I want to go to a jolly party!'

We all watched the new fourth-year's expression as she wrote swiftly, and at length. Stan murmured, 'Looks as if party's coming to us, lad. But, jolly?'

The accident was less than a mile away. A heavy commercial van had skidded onto a pavement, into a rush-hour 'bus queue and crashed on into a shop window. The driver was killed outright. Thirty-four people were injured, fifteen seriously.

Stan rang his wife while we waited for the first ambulance. It arrived at ten to six. It was twenty to eleven before we were empty again.

179

Stan crumpled his limp mask into a paper ball. 'And we needed seven-a-side.' He beckoned Peter and Dave. 'You two get off.' And when they said they would rather wait for us to finish the notes, 'Any more ruddy mutiny and I'll pull rank, change the rota, and there'll be no early half-days Saturday for either of you. You've your lovely lass waiting, Peter, and this'll be toughest on her seeing she's not in the trade, though it'll teach her what to expect once you're wed. Best get over before she changes her mind. You too, young Dave. Out from under my feet! Feet!' He fell into a chair. 'I can stand the blood, the muck, the ruin of me social life, and a diet of bridge rolls and sausages on sticks for the next month—but I can't stand me fallen arches!' He propped an elbow on the desk and smiled, wearily. 'I'd chuck you out, Cath, if I thought I'd get away with it.' He picked up a 'phone. 'Harry? S.A.O. Orthopaedic Theatre finished yet? On the last chap now? Which one's that? Him? No. He'll not take long. Thanks.'

George helped with the notes. Hamish Geddes and the medic. students helped Dolly and Henty with the cleaning, clearing and re-stocking as the student nurses had had to be sent off, protesting. The place was straight by half-past eleven and Dolly stayed on and came in with fresh tea and some rather stale biscuits as we finished. 'Sorry, but these are all we've got in our tin.'

Joss knocked on the open office door. 'May I come in?'

Stan offered him a saucerless cup. 'Make yourself at home! You're one of the family.'

'Thanks.' Joss smiled at me as he sat down. He looked as weary as the other men, but there was no weariness in his smile. 'All go, ain't it?'

'If there's one thing I can't abide,' said Stan, 'it's a dull moment. Repair shop packed it in for the night?'

'Quarter of an hour ago.'

'How'd they make out?'

'They should all do,' said Joss slowly, 'but some'll take a bit of time. How was it here?'

I said, 'Bit nasty.'

'That's right,' said Stan, 'but could've been nastier. We packed 'em all off breathing, which is more than I thought we'd do when some came in.'

George said, 'And tomorrow's New Year's Eve.'

'Brace up, lad,' said Stan kindly. 'Comes round every year. So this time next year when you've got my job you'll know what to expect.' George went purple. 'Didn't you know you were in the running for it?'

I looked at Dolly looking at her cup. 'Actually,' muttered George, 'one—hoped.'

'Dead sensible,' said Joss and Stan nodded.

I did not say anything as Miss Mackenzie was in the doorway. I stood up, quickly. 'I'm sorry we're so late, Sister. We are just going.' The others had risen. 'Er—would you like a cup of tea?'

From her expression I was offering her whisky. 'At this hour—yes—I think I would, thank you, Sister.'

Dolly fetched a cup and saucer. I gave Miss Mackenzie my chair, Stan gave me his and sat on the desk when we all sat down again. He asked, 'Emergencies quiet, Miss Mackenzie?'

'Just now, Mr Lawson. Quite a busy night all round. I only stepped in to say goodbye to Sister and'—she was smiling—'Mr Desmond. St Martha's will miss you both.'

I had never been so glad Joss was a Benedict's man, and had not been brainwashed by her as a student. He said the right things for us both whilst the rest of us exchanged shocked glances. He did blush like a schoolboy when, with a return to her habitual gravity, Miss Mackenzie said she had heard the patients in the Orthopaedic Unit had circumnavigated the rule forbidding members of the staff to accept presents. 'A specially printed outsize card bearing the crest of St Martha's which they have all signed, I believe?'

181

Joss fingered his collar. 'Yes, Sister.'

' A card can scarcely be termed a present, but I would suggest few presents could give greater satisfaction.' She looked at us all. 'One misses the personal touch in departmental work.'

Stan agreed. 'One doesn't like to be impersonal, but often they've moved on before there's time to remember the names on the labels.'

I said, 'Last time; in Canada; and here; it still feels funny not having patients to say goodbye to.'

Miss Mackenzie said, 'I've no doubt. But I know Mr Desmond will agree that had you not moved them on, there would be a great many less names on his card.'

Joss nodded. 'You couldn't be more right, Sister. We repair them in the Orthopaedic Unit, but this is where the lives are saved.'

She turned to Stan. 'How many have you saved, Mr Lawson? This last year? This last six months? Can you count?' Stan shook his head. 'No,' she added crisply, 'it would need an accountant to give the figure from the numbers you deal with.' And then she said, 'In an Accident Unit you can't hear the voices of your recovering patients, but if you stop and think for a wee while, you should hear the voices of the living who, but for your work, would be dead. A pleasing sound.' She pushed back her chair and we all stood up. 'If you'll kindly give me your keys, Sister, I'll lock up with Sister Jones.' Dolly's expression made Martha's history by evoking Miss Mackenzie's second smile in half an hour. 'It is after midnight, Sister Jones. You have taken over.' She accepted the keys, shook my hand and then Joss's. 'Bring your wife over to see us when you return to St Benedict's, and take Sister home, now. It's been a long day.'

I collected my cloak and the dressing-case with my things for the party from the changing-room. Joss took the case, we said another round of goodbyes and walked slowly down the A.U. corridor, into Emergencies hall by the staff door, and out of the main entrance. We did not speak and he did not reach for my hand until I slung on my cloak and we crossed the hospital yard. 'Do you mind leaving too much, darling?'

I glanced over my shoulder. 'Not with you.'

He laced his fingers through mine. Our hands were cold, but the clasp was warm. 'What do you want to do? Catch the end of the party?'

'Not unless you want to.'

'Not tonight. I just want to be alone with you.'

We walked on to the residents' car park, he put my case on the roof of his car and we both turned instinctively and looked back at the hospital. The theatre blocks were in darkness. The red night lights were on in all the wards, but the corridors and stairwells were brilliantly lit. Ghostly, white-capped figures flitted by the red windows; white-coated figures walked more slowly past the lighted windows and would walk more slowly still as the night went on. In silence, and again it semed instinctively, Joss raised his right hand in the old Roman salute, then we got into the car.

In the darkness he kissed me with passionate gentleness. 'Thanks for this, Cathy. Thanks a lot.'

I kissed him back.

Only the main gates were open at that hour of the night. Joss drew up before the small gate lodge and switched on the inside lights briefly for the porter pressing his face to the window to identify us. He waved us on, we waved back, Joss switched off the interior lights and nosed carefully into the always busy main road. The gate porter sat down again and picked up his mug of tea. He did not come down to shut the gates as that was the entrance used day and night by the ambulances, so the gates always stayed open.

Big Ben chimed the half-hour as we crossed the river.

'Tomorrow,' said Joss, 'tomorow. Last one this side of Jordan.'

We drove on, smiling.